Remembered

Rose of Petrichoria

Book 2

By Katie Hauenstein

For my husband,
who helps me always remember
I am loved and supported.

Table of Contents

Prologue

"No one can never know it was me who opened it, Doctor Quincy. I trust the amount of money I am paying you is enough for you to keep silent," he said as Doctor John Quincy escorted him to her chamber.

"I understand your need for discretion. I have already messed with the cameras. No one will know," Doctor Quincy responded.

The two men walked the rest of the way to the cryogenic chamber in silence. Because the room was on the top floor of the hospital and there was a private elevator, secretly getting in and out so late in the night was not a problem.

Arrangements had been made only between the two men. No one else could know, so no middle man had been used. In fact, if it was not for her delicate health, he would have come in and done it all on his own.

Doctor Quincy punched in the code in the first door, pressed his hand to the print reader for the second door, and finally leaned forward for a retinal scan for the final door. "I will wait here for you. Do you remember your instructions? It is vital you do exactly as I said," Doctor Quincy said.

"I remember."

"The power will shut off shortly, that will be the time to use the manual latch. You must have it open for no longer than a minute. I cannot be sure of the consequences if it is open any longer. The emergency power for her chamber will have turned on by then."

"I know. Her safety is my upmost concern right now."

"With all due respect, no, it is not."

At the doctor's words, he stopped and turned to face him. "Pardon me?"

Doctor Quincy frowned. "I am doing this not for your money, as much as I do appreciate the gesture, but for you. However, there is nothing noble about this. You are concerned for your own feelings; it has nothing to do with her safety. If her safety was your top priority, you would leave her be and move on."

He brought a hand to his own face and ran it down over his mouth, stopping at his chin. "It has been so long since I have seen her. I need to."

Doctor Quincy nodded. "I understand. But you must know this is the only time I will do this. No amount of money will make me do this again. She is too important."

"I know. Thank you, Doctor."

Allowing the door to slide shut, he turned and made his way over to the glass chamber. She was so beautiful with her black hair and fair skin; he felt like he was looking at Snow White. She would be amused with knowing how much she appeared like her favorite fairytale princess.

At the thought, the power shut off. Quickly, he grabbed the latch and threw the lid open, setting a timer at his wrist. Doctor Quincy had said the disease would remain frozen when he opened it, so there was no concern for his own health. With a trembling hand he traced the contours of her face. Her skin was so cold and so soft.

"I miss you, Rose," he said. Glancing at his watch, he noticed that thirty seconds had already passed. "I'm so sorry. It does not look like they are any closer today than they were when they put you in here." His timer went off. Too soon! It was too soon for him.

Bending down, he kissed her. If it really was a fairytale, her eyes would flutter open and she would wrap her arms around him, deepening true love's kiss. But it was not a fairytale. The freezing air that began to surround him reminded him of that.

His timer got louder as more time passed. Finally, Doctor Quincy reopened the door and gestured to him furiously to shut the lid. With one last caress of her cheek, he did as the Doctor ordered. Almost immediately, tiny crystals froze along her skin and the glass.

Before leaving, he placed a palm on the glass and whispered, "I love you, Rose. And, again, I am sorry. I hope you can forgive me when you do wake up someday."

Part I

Chapter 1

The next few days went by quickly. Ella finished out the night with me and went home to Peter and Thomas the next morning. She told me when Peter came back from finding me, he insisted that she and Thomas get out of the city. They went north to the Maple Province and were happy to be back in Petrichoria. At least Peter heeded my warning, despite thinking I was crazy.

My lessons with Doctor Bartholomew continued two days after I woke up, and he came to my room for them. Since I was confined to my bed for the time being, we worked on sitting posture. He tried to stack the books, but was scolded by the nurses when he did. He taught me a little more about our history and culture, and explained the expectations I would need to meet when I became Queen someday.

Mother was in and out a lot. She was very busy getting everything together for the Crowning Coronation. Everything had been planned before I was kidnapped – before I went into my freeze, in fact – but none of the supplies were still in the palace. During her visits, I told her everything that happened to me. Every time she heard something new, she cried.

I offered to stop telling her about my captivity, but she insisted on hearing about it. "A mother must know these things. If it was Harmony, you would want to know, right?" I really liked that about both my parents. They talked with me about my false life as if it was real. Even though we all knew it was only a dream world, it was real to me and it felt good to not feel so guarded all the time.

About a week after awakening from the shooting, Doctor Quincy came to visit me in the evening. He checked my vitals and asked about my pain. "It's manageable," I said. "I've even been walking around my room a bit. Mother said she would walk me down to breakfast in the morning."

"Brilliant, Miriam. Absolutely brilliant," John said as he took a seat.

"Did the bullet go straight through? I know there are stitches on the front and back."

John crinkled his nose and quirked an eyebrow for a moment, then a look of understanding crossed his face. "Oh no, Miriam. Projectile weapons have not been used in ages. It was one of the stronger powered light rifles from what we can tell, but we were not able to find it or the shooter."

"That's unfortunate. About the shooter, I mean. Yay for advanced weaponry." I said the last part in a quiet mock victory voice with clenched fists doing little circles in the air.

It was obvious that he was psychoanalyzing me by the look on his face. "I hope you don't mind, but your mother recounted your story of what happened with Frank."

I shook my head. "No. I don't mind. I told her to tell you because I didn't want to rehash it again."

"That is understandable. Are you doing alright now? I know you are not perfect or even feeling normal, yet, but are you alright?"

I sighed. "I think I'm alright. There's nothing I can do about the King's Test. However, I do wish Council could have been a little patient for the facts of what happened before making such idiotic decisions. At least they regret granting Frank a pardon and insisting he participate in the King's Test – not to mention rigging it so he makes it to the final two Arborians. But they can't undo a decision once it is made; he has to do a whole new bad thing for them to do anything."

He laughed. "I do not think patience is one of their strong suits."

"At least that phrase is still around. I've been having issues using common phrases from my false life that don't translate into this one."

"I will bet the transition has been difficult," John inserted.

"Yes, but I think I'm handling it alright."

He smiled. "You *seem* to be handling things alright."

There was an awkward silence. Standing to his feet, he said, "Well, I'm satisfied with your progress and will let the King and Queen know you're ready for Crowning Coronation. Good night, Miriam."

"Good night."

John walked to the door and I asked him to wait before he left. He turned back around.

"Thank you – for everything. You're right. The transition is very hard, but you have been immensely helpful in making it a litter easier for me."

"You are very welcome, Miriam. I will see you next week for an appointment if I do not see you at the Crowning Coronation before." John walked out the door, closing it behind him.

As he was leaving, I leaned over to the light panel and waved to turn off the light. Feeling very tired, I began to walk from my soft chair to my bed. Hearing a knock at the door, I changed course and shuffled myself over to it. When I opened the door, I yelped. I had been expecting anyone – *anyone* – besides who was there.

"F-F-Frank! I'm – surprised to see you."

Where is my new night Guard. What was his name again?

Frank leaned his shoulder into the doorframe with the stupid grin on his face. He ran his hands through his no-longer-close-cut hair and chuckled. "Yes. I'm sorry I haven't been to visit you sooner. I felt terrible about what happened and I had to get my people home and – no. There aren't any good excuses." He was no longer smiling, but looking apologetic.

I rubbed at my wounded shoulder, which was hurting because my pulse was racing and my muscles were tightening. "Trees and blossoms, Frank. Don't worry about me. I'm *fine*." Unfortunately, I grimaced with pain as I said 'I'm fine' so he probably didn't believe me. I just wanted him to go away and I certainly did *not* want him to come in.

He smirked. "While I'm glad you are picking up on current slang, I'm not happy that you just lied to me."

I smirked back. "Good thing you're not in charge anymore." He looked taken aback, so I laughed a little. "I'm *kidding*, Frank. But, really, I'm doing alright. The pain ebbs and flows and isn't *that* bad. I've even been walking around my room for the last couple days."

His face softened. "You're so much stronger than people give you credit for."

I let out a breathy laugh. "I won't disagree, Frank. Unfortunately, every time a major decision has been made concerning my life, I've either been unconscious or in captivity."

He winced when I said the last part, which I didn't mind. He *should* feel bad about what he did.

"You know, I've asked to be called 'Francis' now."

I tilted my head and folded my arms across my chest. "Are people listening to you?"

10

He shrugged. "Mostly."

"Are you wanting me to start calling you 'Francis' now? I will if you want me to. I would totally understand."

He jumped on his answer before I could even finish my sentence. "Oh no. I still want *you* to call me Frank. Like I said before, it's special." He smiled a crooked smile. It was different from his stupid grin – it looked more genuine.

"Alright, Frank." I let there be a short silence. Praying that he would take the hint, I said, "I hope you don't mind, but I've had a long day with Crowning Coronation planning and Doctor Quincy just left. I'm wanting to get some sleep." I milked it by stretching my good arm up and yawning.

He said, "Oh, of course." But rather than leave like I wanted him to, he took my good arm and draped it over his shoulder so he could help me to the bed.

When I sat on the edge, I involuntarily groaned in relief, suddenly grateful he hadn't left after all. I had not realized just how much I was aching before I sat.

"Is there anything else you need, Miriam?"

Well, since he's already in here ...

"I guess I *am* a little achy. Can you get me one of the pills from the bottle on my table?"

"Yes," he said and scampered off to get one with the glass of water sitting next to it. Though his anger was outstanding when he was angry and his forcefulness insane when we was obsessively trying to make me love him, he was gentle the rest of the time. If I could keep him in that zone, his presence might actually be tolerable.

He handed me both and I took the pill. As he walked to the other side of the room to set down the glass, I laid down on my back and pulled the blankets up over me. I expected him to leave, but, once again, he committed an expectation violation and sat on the edge of my bed. Having a feeling he wouldn't be leaving unless he wanted to, I decided to discuss something he wouldn't want to talk about.

"Have you heard the results from the elections in the provinces for King's Test participants? I was really surprised the farmer from Sequoia won – not that I'm upset about it. It's good that there will be a wide variety of stations represented. They should all be arriving tomorrow."

Frank sat there for a moment, just staring at his folded hands in his lap. It was then that I realized he hadn't touched me at all, besides helping me to the bed, since he had been in my room.

I tried and failed to prop myself up on my elbows so I could look at him, so I just looked at my ceiling. "Is everything alright, Frank? You don't seem yourself."

Your handsy, obsessive self.

He scooted closer so he could see my face and I cooperated, tilting my head. He looked at me with a pained expression. "I was thinking about the first night you were on the island. You said something then that began nagging at me after the negotiation; after you were shot."

I yawned again. I really was getting sleepy. "What's that?"

"You asked me why I hadn't just *talked* to you about my concerns. And the night you passed out from your hunger strike, you said you would have done something about it if I would have just taken you home. Remember?"

I paused, not exactly knowing where this was going. "Of course, I do, Frank. I remember everything from my time there."

There was another awkward silence. "I regret it."

I furrowed my brow. "Regret what?"

He sighed and spread his hands. "Everything. For kidnapping you. For forcing myself on you. For slapping you. For not coming here with you when you wanted me to." He paused, refolded his hands, and looked down to them. "I've also been thinking about us."

I wasn't sure if he was waiting for me to respond or if he was trying to drum up the courage for whatever he was going to say. I was in too much shock from his declarations of regret to respond to his second statement of thought.

"I know you're not really in love with me." I gasped and he quickly added, looking back to me, "It's alright. I understand. You were terrified that day – the day I hit you. You were willing to say or do *anything* to get back here. I would have done the same."

I was about in tears as he continued. "Maybe if I hadn't taken you or forced myself on you or hurt you, you *would have* fallen in love with me naturally, rather than the artificial way I created on that island." He sighed. "It's my own fault." He looked back at his hands.

"Maybe you're right."

He just nodded, still not daring to touch me even a little bit.

I looked at the ceiling again. "I definitely would have said something, though – if you *had* come to me. You know that, right?"

He nodded again and shrugged a shoulder. "I think I was so desperate for us to be heard, that I never even thought to do that, much less consider doing it."

"Hmm." I sighed. "Frank, would you like me to be brutally honest with you?"

I could feel he was looking at me again, but didn't look back.

"Yes, but maybe you can sugar-coat it for me just a little."

I smirked.

'Sugar-coat' is one I can keep.

"Okay. I'll try – I will never forget the hell of being on that island – Of feeling so alone and scared – Of not knowing whether or not I would ever come home – Of fearing how far you would go with forcing yourself on me on any given night."

I looked at him in time to see him grimace. "However – and don't make *me* regret this – I believe in second chances. You've already been pardoned by the Council and you will be living here for a while for the King's Test. Blossoms, we could end up married at the end of it because the choice has even been taken out of Father's hands. We're going to be seeing each other a lot and I would rather not spend that time afraid of you."

"I don't want you to be afraid of me," he said quietly.

"I know. I remember you saying that before, and I believe you meant it then and you mean it now – I forgive you, Frank." I took one of his hands, hoping on all that is good and green that I wouldn't come to regret what I was saying. "I think we should start over again; try to put the past in the past and keep it there. Not forget it; that's not possible, but move on. Do you think we can do that?"

He smirked. "Are you patronizing me?"

I seriously said, "No, of course not. I sincerely want to start over, as ridiculous as it sounds." I shrugged as well as I could laying down. "This time you're not my Guard, you're a participant in the King's Test. If you win me, I will have to learn to like you anyway. Might as well start early."

I smiled, trying to assure him that I meant everything I said – and the crazy thing was that I *did* forgive him. I was still terrified of him and would avoid being alone with him at all costs, but I forgave him. He ended up doing the right thing in the end by agreeing to the negotiations and asking me for forgiveness; I only hoped his request for forgiveness also extended into repentance.

He smiled back, breathing out with a huff of relief. "I would love to start over. Though I want you to know I would never look at you as a prize to be won."

I laughed sardonically. "That's *exactly* what I am, Frank. A prize; my Crown and me. I don't know why I'm saying this to you, of all people, but I'm truly afraid of the results."

"I can make you a promise."

"Yeah? Be careful what you promise, lest you're not able to keep it."

He chuckled. "I'm sure I can keep it. I promise that if I lose, which, let's face it, is a big possibility, I will be your friend as long as you'll have me. And if the winner turns out to be a loser to you, I'll be around to remind you that you are a person, not an object – as a friend, of course."

"Thank you, Frank."

"No. Thank *you*, Miriam. I don't deserve anything you've granted me tonight. You are gracious and kind; truly magnanimous. You have proved yourself to be the Rose of Petrichoria."

Though he was being serious, I couldn't help but bust out laughing. Blossoms, I laughed much harder than I had in a very long time. Apparently, it was contagious because he was soon laughing as well, though I don't know that he understood why I was laughing.

When I calmed down and wiped a tear from my eye, I said, "As much as I love the roses – they really are beautiful and their scent is among my favorites – I don't think that title is *ever* going to grow on me."

Frank crookedly smiled as I yawned shortly after my confession.

"You really should go to sleep, Miriam. What are you doing staying up talking to me?" Smile still on his face, he brought my hand up and kissed my knuckles. It was nothing romantic, just a societal norm.

"I'm crazy. That's why. Go away, Frank."

He laughed as he stood up and walked to the open doorway.

Just as he crossed the threshold, He turned his head to look back at me and said, "Good night, Miriam."

"Good night, Frank. Oh, and tell my night Guard to do his job."

As he closed the door behind him, my eyes became heavy quickly. Soon enough, I fell asleep without feeling some form of despair for the first night since I had woken up from my false life and was thrown into my real one.

Chapter 2

A week later, I was standing in front of my full length mirror with Adele, Christine, and Bell close by. I kept my face straight as I carefully examined my appearance. It was my Crowning Coronation and I had to look perfect.

My simple tiara sat before an updo of long and intertwining curls which were masterfully done by Christine. The makeup Bell had applied was elegant. There had been no need for foundation because, as Bell said, there wasn't a single blemish – after saying that, she went on for the next fifteen minutes about her oily skin. My cheeks were rosy and my lips were a shade of deep red, applied with lip stick and liner. On my eyes, there was a light cream color between my brows and lids. A pretty olive green shadow that had a gold sheen at certain angles amplified my green eyes.

Adele had outdone herself with the design of the gown. My skirt was huge – like something straight from the Rococo era – and made of the softest silk. So the colors of the embellishments would seem more vibrant, the gown was chocolate brown. The bodice had a square neck beginning at the edge of my clavicle with elbow-length sleeves; it was tight, like the dress I had worn at the ball, but not too tight, since I was still a little sore. Embroidered on every edge – bodice, sleeves, and hem – were green vines and leaves with tiny bright red roses. At the elbows, lace in the same color of green, created a small bell.

I wore no gloves this time because of tradition, though I did let them know I would like to have them whenever it was possible. They made me feel like the Princess I was. Rather than high heels, my feet were adorned with simple, yet graceful chocolate brown flats – if I was going to need to run, I was *not* removing my shoes this time.

I turned away from the mirror to face the ladies who were anxiously awaiting my praise or pout. Keeping a straight face until the silence became awkward, I said, "This dress, ladies, is – hmm – how should I put it?"

I looked up to the ceiling with only my eyes and placed my index finger on the side of my chin as if considering a gentle way to put it. "Ah. Yes. This dress is – absolutely extravagant." I smiled, then and the ladies rejoiced. "Truly, it is a beautiful gown and I am honored to wear something so beautiful for my Crowning Coronation."

Then, I was smothered with hugs and declarations of my beauty. As an afterthought, the hugs were followed with curtsies. I was beginning to get used to it; the curtsies and bows came with the job.

Just as my assistants finished their curtsies, a knock sounded on my door. Knowing it was Louis to escort me to the ballroom for the ceremony, I hurried over and opened the door. Because today was ceremoniously special, Louis was dressed in the Royal Arborian Guard's forest green dress uniform.

"Well, you look rather dapper today, Sir Louis."

"Thank you, Your Highness." Louis cleared his throat. "This is a little awkward and completely unprofessional, but I have a request of you."

Stepping out of the room the rest of the way and closing the door behind me, I quirked a brow because Louis never asked for anything, I said, "This is intriguing. What is your request?"

"You see, my wife did not get drawn in the lottery for tickets to see you coroneted today, but they wanted to see you and bless you for everything you have done. They are waiting at the main entrance. It would be a great honor for them. Would you please come meet them?"

I beamed. "Of course I will! It would be lovely to meet them. I am sure they are wonderful."

I was right. His family was, unsurprisingly, wonderful. His wife couldn't stop thanking me for making sure Louis received a promotion and his daughter looked like her head would explode from happiness.

After we met them, we made our way to the main ballroom in silence. I was very nervous as I considered everything my Crowning Coronation would mean. I was about to be recognized as the Crown Princess, deemed mature and ready to rule, should the need arise. After the coronation, there would be a great feast and a ball.

The next day, the process of determining who was most suited to become the King of Arboria would begin. It would be the official beginning of the King's Test. I would meet each one of the twenty gentlemen individually when we retried the Introduction Event.

That was all assuming everything went as planned this time around.

Third time's a charm, right?

I shook my head to get my thoughts back on the matter at hand, but it was already too late by the time I succeeded. I was looking at the beautiful doors, shaking in my flats.

Taking a deep breath, I said, "Here I go."

As Louis opened the door and I stepped inside, everyone seated stood to face me. The action reminded me of walking in as the bride of David Dutch for our wedding. I had not had any more visions since I woke from being shot, I realized. I wondered if he was done visiting me.

Walking down the aisle, I politely nodded in acknowledgement as each row bowed or curtsied when I passed by them. Father and Mother were standing on a pretty wooden platform and seeing them helped me relax.

Approaching them, I knelt on one knee, as I had been instructed to do. Keeping my head lowered, Father began the ceremony.

"Citizens of Arboria! We have come together this day to acknowledge Princess Miriam Petrichoria of Arboria is fully prepared to one day be Queen of this great kingdom. Today, we will coronate her Crown Princess."

I looked up to him.

"Princess Miriam, do you swear your loyalty and service to the people of Arboria? To make every decision based on the well-being of those people rather than on your own desires?"

"I do."

"Do you swear to work cordially with the elected Province Delegates who will make you aware of the opinions and circumstances of the people of Arboria?"

"I do."

"Do you swear to accept the highest scored participant of the King's Test? To honor him as your husband and support him as your King?"

This part had been changed because of the situation the Council had put us in.

"I do."

"Please rise and face those in attendance today."

I rose and turned as gracefully as possible.

"Princess Miriam, I first present you with your scepter, the Rosa Illuminata. May it always be a reminder of your responsibility to rule with all your heart and soul."

Mother held the scepter out to me horizontally and I accepted it. Just as she had said the first night I was at Evergreen Palace, it was beautiful. Unsurprisingly, it was solidly made of rose gold. Circling from the bottom to the crowning stone was a green vine of some metal. On top was a large, transparent pink stone that had been carved into a rose. At certain angles, it appeared to glow with an ethereal light.

"You will next receive your scale. May it always be a reminder that you will rule with grace and justice."

Mother held out an old-fashioned scale, also made of rose gold and I accepted it in my other hand.

"Finally, I gladly place upon your head your new tiara. May it always be a reminder of this day and all you have vowed before these witnesses."

Behind me, I felt Father place my new tiara on my head. I was dying to see it.

"Citizens of Arboria! I present to you Crown Princess Miriam Petrichoria of Arboria! Please rise and demonstrate your blessing on this Crowning Coronation!"

Every person in the room stood and either bowed or curtsied. Some were smiling. Some were crying with joy. When they rose, they yelled in unison.

"Long live Crown Princess Miriam, the Rose of Petrichoria!"

Chapter 3

All the King's Test participants were in attendance at the Crowning Coronation Feast. Because my Introduction Event had gone horribly wrong two times in a row, I had requested there *not* be a ball this time around.

Mother and I had decided that rather than have the herald introduce the new Arborian participants, they would each introduce themselves at the Crowning Coronation Feast. The Princes were also there, but since they had already been introduced, they would not get to approach me that evening – Although Prince Harrison and I exchanged glances and smiles more than once throughout the evening. Frank, obviously, would not need introduction either. The interviews would begin the following morning since there were so many participants.

Dinner had been eaten and we were all sipping at wine when Mother announced the beginning of the introductions. I sat a little straighter as I looked down the row of men I had been eyeing all evening.

The Arborian men rose and made a line. The first approached and bowed to kiss my hand. He was a little shy of six feet tall with side swept black hair and blue eyes. "Princess Miriam, I am Robert Casey of Petrichoria." No one would be saying anything beyond their names that night. After everyone introduced themselves, we would all be going to bed.

The next man looked like something straight out of a superhero movie. He was large, like a body builder, with a long blond ponytail tied at the nape of his neck. "I am Jonathan Stone of Cedar, Princess Miriam." He kissed my hand.

"Princess Miriam, I am Saul Stone of Birch," said the second muscular man of the evening. He was similar in stature to Jonathan, but had buzzed blonde hair. I briefly remembered they were cousins as he bent and kissed my hand.

"Princess Miriam, I am Henry Braeburn of Sequoia." The farmer I had brought up when talking with Frank introduced himself. He was tanned from his hours in the sun and a glint of humor sparkled in his green eyes when he kissed my hand.

A young man with purposefully disheveled dark blond hair came over and said, "I am Percival Andrews of Oak, Princess Miriam." As he kissed my hand, I noticed Ella wipe a tear from her eye and wondered what she was thinking.

Here comes a rock star…

"I am Lucas Flowers of Willow, Princess Miriam," said a man wearing more jewelry than I was. His straight medium-length brown hair swept over my thumb as he kissed my hand. If we had been back in the twenty-first century, I would have pictured the grey-eyed man surrounded by ladies as he wooed them with beautiful lyrics and minor chords on a guitar.

A sharp bespectacled gentleman with a tight black bun high upon his head bowed and kissed my hand after saying, "Princess Miriam, I am Alan Daniels of Alder."

Tenor. I wonder if I can have them sing to me as one of their tests…

"I am Troy Gold of Juniper, Princess Miriam," the next gentleman introduced himself. He had short blond hair and bright blue eyes. He gingerly took my hand and kissed it.

Finally, the last man came up and I saw Peter and Ella smiling like deer in a berry bush.

Must be Maple.

"I am Samuel Harper of Maple, Princess Miriam." He was the only red-head out of the twenty men present and his caramel-colored eyes looked at me as if I was the most beautiful thing he had ever seen. He swallowed hard and his hand shook when he took mine and kissed it. When he made his way back to his seat, he looked over to Peter and Ella, who gave him approving nods.

They know him personally. I wonder what all that is about.

It was my turn to speak and end the evening's events. "Princes and Gentlemen of the King's Test, Dukes, Duchesses, Delegates, and fellow Arborians. Thank you for joining me this evening in celebrating my Crowning Coronation. I am honored to serve this great kingdom and hope I can do so as well as my father and mother have for so many years.

"I look forward to the coming months when I will get to know each one of the participants of the King's Test personally and come out the other side with Arboria's new Crown Prince.

"Please be safe on your trips home or to your rooms this evening. Good night."

Tomorrow is a new adventure for my real life. I hope I will start remembering some of it soon.

Chapter 4

"Good Morning, Crown Princess! Time to pucker up!" Adele woke me up the day after my Crowning Coronation with way too much enthusiasm for six in the morning.

"Stll Mphrum, Dll. Shut pp nd lt m slipp," I mumbled face-first into my pillow as Adele made kissy sounds.

"I cannot understand you when you talk into your pillow," she said matter-of-factly.

Groggily, I looked up at my assistant, who was smirking at my rough appearance. "I said, 'I am still Miriam, Adele. Shut up and let me sleep.' Just because my title changed, it does not mean I want you calling me by it." Getting those who worked closest with me to stop referring to me by my title was a never-ending battle. I smashed my face back into my pillow and snuggled into my blankets.

Laughing, she walked over and yanked my cozy blanket off my body, making me shiver in the wintery cold air. Curling up into fetal position, and ignoring the no-contraction protocol, I said, "Carp, Adele! Why isn't the heat on in here?"

"Carp, Miriam?" She looked amused.

"Ugh. Fine! I will get up!" I sat up quickly and dropped my legs over the edge. Years of being woken up by Harmony taught me that it was the quickest way for me to wake up in the morning. It was kind of like ripping off a band-aid. The longer I dallied in bed, the more painful it was to actually get up.

"Excellent," Adele said, chin up and striding to my closet.

"Pants, please!" I shouted as I stretched and padded over to the bathroom to freshen up for the day.

"Nope!" she simply replied. The woman loved dresses. Trying to get her to let me wear pants was like trying to pull a stump out of the ground bare-handed.

"Remember who pays you, Adele! You are much too peppy this morning!"

"King Aaron?" she laughed, then began humming as she made her decision on what *dress* I would wear.

"Dresses. I thought this was supposed to be the twenty-third century. I just want a frakking pair of blue jeans," I muttered as I put the toothpaste on my toothbrush.

Right as I began scrubbing, I heard my holocomm beeping in the room. Adele rushed over to answer it for me. After a short conversation, she peeked into the bathroom. "Speaking of the King, he wanted me to remind you that you have a short meeting with him and Duchess Elleouise this morning before meeting the men."

I groaned and spit. "What? Is he going to give me tips? Like how to kiss twenty different people and still have feeling in my lips at the end of the day?"

Adele laughed and shrugged as I rinsed. "I do not know and it is not my business. I am almost ready for you, Miriam."

I waved her off as I spit the water into the sink. "Yeah, yeah, yeah. I will be there in a minute." Adele giggled as she walked away again. I liked her. Even though she had too much amusement at my hatred of early mornings, she was a real person. Out of all the staff at Evergreen Palace, Adele probably treated me the closest to normal.

While I was sure Ella was my best friend before my stint of ten years in cryogenic freeze, we had yet to really reconnect. Part of that was probably because she married my boyfriend, Peter, while I was sleeping. Personally, it didn't really bother me too much anymore. I didn't remember my relationship with him and they were happy. Ella was the one still living with guilt; no matter what I said, I couldn't pull her out of it.

However, Peter was on my short list of people I tried to avoid at all costs. Knowing I wouldn't remember him, he took advantage of the fact that he reminded me of my late husband from my false life and kissed me after I woke up. I had made it abundantly clear I would be no man's mistress and he needed to be faithful to his wife. As far as I could tell, he had not given up on me yet.

Adele shouted from the other room, "I am waiting, Miriam! You have a long day ahead of you and the King wants to see you before everything begins at 8:00."

I mumbled complete nonsensical syllables as I walked out of the bathroom with a clean face, deodorant applied, and smelling of roses. "Let us get this over with." I said in a yawn.

She held up a beautiful green satin A-line dress with a heart-shaped bodice. I smiled at her and she said, "I knew I would get a smile for choosing satin. There is no reason for you to be totally uncomfortable all day." I laughed at how well she already knew me after only a few short months.

"At least I will be comfortable in my clothing. My lips and dignity? Those are going out the window today."

Over the next half hour, she helped me dress, straightened my hair, and applied some light make-up. The dress had a small pocket at the hem for me to store a little tube of lip gloss, which I thought was ingenious, considering how I was going to be spending my day.

Finally, she placed my new tiara on my head. I had admired it the previous night before going to sleep, but couldn't get over how truly lovely it was. It was made in rose gold, to match my scepter and scale, I assumed, and the band was thicker than my Princess tiara. Vines, thorns and tiny roses wove an intricate pattern delicately over the top. It really was beautiful.

After one more quick examination in the mirror, I said goodbye to Adele, and Louis escorted me to Father's office. As we passed the second floor, I glanced into the Dining Hall, where the participants of the King's Test awaited their turn in my rose maze.

In the brief moment I looked, I could see a couple of them sizing each other up. Most notably, Prince Harrison was shooting daggers with his eyes at Frank from across the room and Prince Phineas was glaring at Prince Mamoru.

The level of testosterone I'm going to have to endure over the next couple months is going to be excruciating.

Louis caught me rolling my eyes as I turned away from the room and smiled. I noticed his smile and asked him, "Are all men like that, Louis, or am I just lucky?" He laughed, but didn't answer my rhetorical question.

When we arrived at Father's office, he pushed the button to slide open the door and I walked in. "Good morning, Father, Ella, Peter – wait – what?"

I gaped at the unexpected member in our meeting. "What is Peter doing here?" I tried not to say his name with venom, but I was not sure how successful I was.

Father smiled innocently and Peter matched his expression. "Peter participated during the first round before your freeze. I thought maybe his insight might be useful."

"With all due respect, I would rather take advice on lip gloss application from a duck."

"That is a weird insult, Rose, and there is not really any respect in it," Peter said, replacing his innocent smile with a pout.

"Like I said, 'with all *due* respect.'"

Ella laughed and Peter gave her a dirty look, which made her laugh harder. "Really, Peter. You can't blame her. You have kind of been a jerk since she's woken up."

Peter shook his head and smiled despite himself. Father just watched the interaction with delight painted all over his face.

"Alright, alright," Peter said and Ella finally stopped laughing. "Look, I know we have gotten off on the wrong foot –"

"Feet," I corrected and smiled despite *myself.*

He chuckled. "Semantics. I'm really sorry how things were when you woke up, but I was kind of hoping that after I found you out in the woods with the search team and took your advice about Ella and Thomas that you would ease up a bit on me."

Father looked at me with a puzzled look on his face. I had not told him anything about the premonition concerning the safety of Peter's family – or any other premonition, for that matter.

I bit the corner of my lower lip and considered what Peter said. When he and I talked during his attempted rescue, I had told him about a vision I had of seeing Ella and Thomas' graves and asked that he get them out of the city for a while. When I saw Ella next, she told me he had taken my advice.

Sighing in defeat, I pointed at him with a stiff finger and said, "Alright. One chance. If you are a jerk, you're gone. Got it?"

Peter smiled stupidly. "Anything you say, oh Rose of Petrichoria."

I rolled my eyes, then returned my attention to Father. "I think I'm done with that. Is that what you needed to see me about?"

"It was part of the reason, but not all. I had a meeting with the Council late last night about the sheer number of men we have participating. It's unprecedented. We have decided –"

"Hold on. Correct me if I'm wrong, but shouldn't I be involved in the Council meetings when I am not unconscious or in captivity somewhere?"

"Yes, but not in regards to the King's Test. I am sorry, Rose. I know that this is very difficult for you. When I told you about it the first time, you were thirteen; you had several years to get used to it. Unfortunately, you do not have that this time around."

I nodded and gestured for him to continue. He cleared his throat. "Right. As I was saying, we have decided that after you report on your interviews, Peter, Ella, and I will decide on five Princes to cut and five Arborians to cut."

My mouth dropped. "No offense, but aren't Peter and Ella a little biased as far as the participants are concerned?"

Father quirked a brow, but Peter and Ella shifted in their seats. "What do you mean?" Father asked.

"I saw them react for two of the Arborians last night. One was Percival of Oak and the other was Samuel of Maple."

Father looked over to them. "Explain."

Ella spoke up this time. "Percival of Oak, we don't know. I only reacted because he is – from – Oak. I will admit, though, that we know Samuel."

"I see," Father said as he leaned back in his chair.

"I don't. What does Percival being from Oak have to do with anything?" I asked.

"We had a good friend from Oak. Stephan. He was close to you, like a brother – he died when the Daze mutations were unleashed on the Noble houses. We were all very close." Ella looked down at her hands. Shrugging, she said, "Percival doesn't look like Stephan at all; he just reminded me of someone we lost."

"Oh," I uttered. I felt bad. Not sad, but guilty. One of my best friends had died a horrible death and I didn't even remember his name or where he was from.

Father bit his thumb. "The fact that you *do* know Samuel, though, does present a problem. I am afraid you will only be able to help eliminate the Princes."

"Gladly," Peter said under his breath. I thought he might still be jealous that I had begun the Welcoming Ball with Prince Harrison rather than him. Or maybe that I seemed much happier to see Prince Harrison and Prince Phineas during the rescue mission.

"What about Frank, Father?" I asked.

"What about him," Father answered my question with a question. I narrowed my eyes to show him I was annoyed because I knew he understood what I meant.

"Can he be one of the five Arborians eliminated? I would really rather not spend the rest of my life with a man who kidnapped me and held me hostage for two months before trying to overthrow you."

"Here, here!" piped in Ella.

"Unfortunately, no. Remember, it's rigged so he makes it to the final two Arborians," Father said.

I huffed. "Really, it is unbelievable that the Council is letting a traitor compete for the Crown."

"I agree, but there is nothing to be done about it."

After a minute or two of silence, Louis rung the door chime and Father admitted him. "Your Majesty, Your Highness, Your Lordship and Ladyship, the participants are ready for you. They are getting – restless." Louis struggled over that last word, which made me wonder what in the world was going on.

Without waiting for Father or Ella, I threw my shoulders back and marched out of the office to the Core where I found my twenty suitors yelling at each other.

Chapter 5

It was a veritable war zone in the Core. My suitors were in two lines facing each other like kids playing Red Rover on the playground. Their maturation at the moment was probably on the same level as grade schoolers, as well.

Breathing from my diaphragm and lowering my pitch just a tad so it would carry, I shouted, "What in the name of all that is green and good is going on out here?"

Father and Ella caught up as the men all stopped yelling and hurriedly reformed into one straight line standing at attention. I heard Ella snicker behind me. No one answered my question.

Quieting my voice and pacing the line in front of me, I said, "I think you may have misunderstood me. I did not simply want you all to stop bucking antlers, I want an answer. You have all been brought here to participate in the *King's Test*, for blossom's sake.

"When I came out here, I expected to meet with the shining gentlemen who introduced me to themselves either last night or at the ball three months ago. So, please, someone explain to me why I found each and every one of you lined up against each other and shouting like toddlers throwing a temper tantrum."

I knew a temper tantrum when I saw one, too. Harmony was an expert at being a little drama queen.

The line of men stayed silent and I was reminded of a time in choir when I was a child. Someone in the classroom had put a whoopee cushion in the padding of the piano bench and the director was not laughing. He had asked who did it and no one spoke up or pointed to a little boy named Matthew who had done the deed. We all ended up punished by having to write octaves in the key of C on sheet music for the whole class time.

I pinched the bridge of my nose as I tried to come up with something as clever for this group of men. Finally, Prince Mamoru stepped forward. I quirked a brow. I had yet to hear him utter a single word, so I wondered what he was going to say.

After bowing, Prince Mamoru said, "Crown Princess, my greatest apologies on behalf of us all. You are absolutely correct. We should have better heads on our shoulders."

"Indeed," I replied and waited when he didn't continue immediately. "Why were you yelling, Prince Mamoru?"

"I am afraid one Prince insulted an Arborian for being low-class and things snowballed from there." He stepped back into the line. That was the only explanation I was going to get.

Very diplomatic.

I glanced over my shoulder at Father to see if he wanted to take charge, but he only nodded and motioned for me to carry on. I cleared my throat.

"Let me make something abundantly clear, Princes and Arborians. This kingdom is ruled not only by our elected Delegates and not only by our Royalty. We rule together. We respect each other.

"If you cannot respect one another as equal participants in this King's Test, then we have a problem. If anyone is caught taking part in anything like this in the future, I will ask the Council to remove you from participation on the grounds that you are unfit to rule. Am I understood?"

Every man in the line, no matter how big or small, nodded his head sheepishly in understanding. How sincere in their humility they were being, I didn't know, but they at least understood their places.

"Very well, I will hand things over to Father and my Crown Princess' Maiden, Ella. I will see each of you at some point today and at dinner this evening." I started at one end of the line, walked to the other side and behind to go to my rose maze.

Seeing the men arguing like that made me extremely nervous, not only for the future of Arboria, but for my future as well. David was the measure of a man they had to work towards and it was not looking good for them.

What were they thinking getting into an argument like that? Right in the middle of the Core! Did they even consider the kind of impression that would make on me? Not that it really matters. I don't know why I even have to participate in the King's Test now that the decision is purely objective. At least the Council is granting Father the right to eliminate ten men tonight.

Chapter 6

Alan Daniels of Alder

Making my way through the maze, I nibbled at my thumb nail. I knew it was a dirty habit, but I had never broken it and it helped me calm down. Finally, I made it to my sofa swing and plopped myself down upon it.

Ugh. I plopped. Doctor Bartholomew would have my head if he knew. I can hear him now. "Princesses do not plop, Miriam. Sit the correct way ten times, please."

Smiling at my mental imitation of my tutor, I tilted my head back and watched the rain pelt the glass ceiling of my garden. Actually, all the walls were made of glass. I designed it that way so I could enjoy sitting in the rain without getting wet – or so I was told.

I was annoyed and frustrated about the day ahead of me. It was incredible to me how this kingdom could be advanced in so many ways, yet still maintain such an archaic and strange tradition. In my false life, first kisses were precious. A lady *never* kissed on the first date. Apparently, in my real life, my father wanted me to kiss twenty men I did not know at all.

After a few minutes of stewing in anger, my first suitor arrived. Alan Daniels, his black hair in a long braid this time, shifted on his feet in the archway. "Hello, Crown Princess."

"Hello, Alan. Please, call me Miriam."

"Alright."

Alan stopped shifting, but he still stood in the archway, looking extremely nervous.

"There is no need to be nervous, Alan. I know you are the first today and that cannot be easy."

I really hate that I can't use contractions. How I miss them in my everyday life. You never realize how much you miss something until you lose it.

Alan took a deep breath and came to sit by me. "You have a very beautiful garden, Miriam."

"Thank you. I like to come here when it is raining so I can watch it."

As he took my hand, he cleared his throat. The anxiety I felt at his contact caused my hands to grow clammy. "It is nice to see that you appreciate nature so much. It is very important to me."

"Nature? How do you mean? Is it not important to all of us?"

He smiled and ran his hand down his side braid. "It should be, but it is not held as important as it should be. I believe the trees we surround our homes and buildings with are alive, beyond the scientific way that we all accept. They have souls, Miriam."

Oh great. Here we go.

"The trees in my home have always been treated as extensions of my family," he continued. "We speak to them about our days, spend time with them, you know, things you would do with any family member."

"Do they speak back to you?" I asked, trying really hard to hide my amusement. A smile cracked through, but he just smiled back and moved closer to me.

Carp! His time is running short. He's going to kiss me soon.

"No. We have not figured out how to understand them yet. I know it sounds strange, Miriam, but it is true. I hope that if I end up your King, I can help you and other people see the veracity of what I say."

That must have been romantic to him in some strange way because that was when he kissed me. It was soft and sweet, but his breath tasted slightly of bark and it made me wonder if he had been sampling my tree family. When he pulled away, he smiled and left. Shortly after he had gone, Ella yelled that his time was up and she was sending in the next man. Wiping his weirdness off my mouth, I considered how terrible he would be for Arboria as King.

Sorry, Alan, but you are definitely going home if I have anything to say about it. We don't need to give a wacko the Crown.

Prince Alexander of Scandinavia

The happiest man participating in the King's Test bounded in next. His blond curls bounced and his smile was so big, his sea-green eyes were almost closed.

"Crown Princess Miriam! I found you! What an ingenious maze!" He grabbed my hands and pulled me up into a spinning embrace. I could not help but laugh at his exuberance.

"Thank you, Prince Alexander. Please, call me Miriam. Especially if you are going to be dancing around with me like that."

Alexander laughed as he swooped me up so I was cradled in his arms. "Alright. Then you will call me Alex." He set me back down onto the sofa and sat close to me.

"Miriam, I have been so excited for the King's Test to begin so I can prove myself to you."

Still breathing a bit rapidly because of all the excitement, I said, "Well, today is the only day you need to prove anything to me. After today, everything is objective."

There was a moment of silence between us as we both calmed our heart rates. I tilted my head back with closed eyes and listened to the rain.

He took my hand with one of his and leaned over me to cradle my head and lift it with his other.

Well, that was quick.

When I opened my eyes, I saw his brow furrowed. Because it didn't match his body language at all, it confused me. "Did I do something to upset you?" I asked and swallowed hard.

"No. Not you." He softened his expression. "None of this is fair to you. I am sorry that this is the way things are for you."

"How do you mean?"

"This – King's Test. It is appalling to me that this would be the way a father would treat his daughter." His thumb stroked my cheek as he spoke.

"If it is so appalling to you, why are you here?"

"I want to give you a chance at a happy life. You deserve a good man and Heaven knows that not all the men here are good men."

"You – you came here specifically for me? You had a choice?"

He chuckled dryly. "Yes. I had a choice. In my kingdom, the Princes and Princesses can marry whomever they choose. We get to marry for love."

"That must be nice," I breathed. His face was getting close to mine and he smiled. "You would give up love for me? You do not even know me."

"I know *of* you. I know you have compassion for your people, and you long for justice and grace to be a part of your reign when you become Queen. Those are qualities in a woman I can find myself loving." His gaze moved to my lips. "It does not hurt that you are the most beautiful woman I have ever laid eyes on."

At that, he closed the gap between us and kissed me. He released my hand and moved his free hand to my upper back to pull me closer to him. I couldn't help but wonder if he was so concerned about my treatment why he was taking advantage this particular tradition. He didn't *have* to kiss me.

I knew I would be hearing pretty words all day; I had prepared myself for it, but I was moved by what he had said, even if a kiss *had* followed it. No one had said anything like it to me – well, except Frank, but he was insane, so that didn't count. There was something wonderful and beautiful about Alex and I found myself hoping he made it far into the King's Test.

He stopped our passionate kiss and gave me another peck before resting his forehead against mine. "I will see you this evening at dinner, Miriam." He slowly released me from his hold and gave me a kiss on the cheek before leaving me, stunned.

Prince Estevan of Amazonia, Saul Stone of Birch, and Troy Gold of Juniper

A good while later, I heard Ella yell out, "Prince Estevan, time's up!" Then, I heard a masculine groan. Apparently, Prince Estevan couldn't find his way through the maze. Later on down the line, Saul Stone and Troy Gold couldn't find their way either.

I pumped my fist. Three kisses I didn't have to offer, though I did feel a little sorry for them. Because of the objective turn this King's Test had taken, they would most likely be automatically disqualified.

Even if they wouldn't be automatically disqualified, I would probably recommend them for elimination. The maze wasn't too difficult and it didn't say much for their capability for strategy if they couldn't make it through a simple maze.

Perhaps it was a harsh judgment, but since there were twenty men competing and the rest were able to find their way, I didn't really see a reason to hold on to them. I told myself that during my meeting with Father, Peter, and Ella, I would put them up for elimination.

Prince Harrison of Southland

After having tons of time to think about Alex, since Prince Estevan and the others didn't make it through the maze, I was relaxed and ready for the next man to come through the archway. I had figured out that the order was probably alphabetical, but I didn't want to use the brain power to figure out who would be next.

"Howdy, Crown Princess."

"Prince Harrison!" I actually leaped out of my seat and threw myself into his arms. His giant arms wrapped around me and he put his cheek on my head with a chuckle.

"Well, this is a surprise," he said. "Please, call me Harrison."

"You call me Miriam," I said quietly and pulled away slightly, remaining in his arms. "This should not be too much of a surprise, Harrison. You were one of my rescuers. Who knows where I would be right now if it was not for you."

He smirked. "Well, I could not let that devil have such a precious woman." His gaze became serious. "Ever since the night you woke up from your freeze and I saw you climbing the stairs in the Core, I knew you were special. Then, you sent us away when we tried to rescue you. I knew you were a strong woman from the stories that have been told about you, but you have surpassed any expectations I ever had of you already."

I laughed quietly. "I wish I could have proven it some other way."

Harrison traced my jawline with his fingertips. "Me, too. I was so worried about you."

"Me, too."

Harrison laughed. He slowly lowered his head and tipped mine up to meet him – he was *so* tall. Tentatively, he brushed his lips against mine. I opened my eyes, not realizing I had even closed them, and saw his heavy-lidded gaze with those Kona-blue eyes. Smiling, I wrapped my hands around his neck and pulled him in for a deeper kiss.

I wasn't sure what it was about Harrison, but I felt connected to him. The fact that his eyes were so similar to David's couldn't escape me and he had come to save me when I was kidnapped. When we danced, it felt like we belonged together.

What had me nervous was that I thought I might be falling in love with him, which would be tragic.

If only I could choose, I would choose you.

Harrison smiled into the kiss as if he could read my thoughts and pulled me closer to him.

Can he read my thoughts? If I have premonitions why couldn't someone else be able to read minds? No. That's crazy.

We finally stopped when Ella called out that his time was up. Pressing his forehead against mine, he whispered, "Miriam, you may just be the end of me." Then he kissed me one last time and left.

Henry Braeburn of Sequoia

"Hello, Henry. Please call me Miriam." I decided to nip the request in the bud to save time. Henry seemed taken aback by the request, but smiled and told me he would. I had returned to my seat and patted the cushion next to me. Obligingly, he sat next to me, flipping his side-parted golden brown hair to the left out of his eyes.

The sun had decided to part the clouds for a while and it reflected sun-bleached red highlights in his hair. I looked at his tan face, clear green eyes, bright teeth, and wide smile. When that smile let out a light laugh, I realized I had been unabashedly checking him out and I felt heat rise to my cheeks.

"It's alright. I get it all the time," he said in an unboastful manner. I could tell he was just trying to help me relax.

"I do, too," I responded and Henry laughed.

"I'm sure you do. You have been declared the fairest of them all over and over again."

"Ha! Clever you. How did you know Snow White was my favorite fairytale?"

"I didn't. You just look like you could be related what with the black hair, pale skin, and red lips."

I smiled. "Well, thank you. Luckily, I do not have an evil stepmother who wants my heart carved from me."

"I would save you. I would do a *much* better job than seven dwarfs."

"I know you would."

We swung in amiable silence for a few moments and he held my hand. Sighing, I lay my head on his shoulder. It did not surpass my notice that his speech had been very informal with me and I liked it; I liked that this man was not afraid to be himself with me.

"Miriam, can I confess something to you?"

"Mmm-hmm."

"I'm not going to kiss you right now."

Lifting my head from his shoulder, I tilted my head and looked at him with confusion. "You just said I was fairest of them all. Why do you not want to kiss me?"

He chuckled. "Oh. It's not that. I really do *want* to kiss you."

"Then why not?"

"I want it to mean something when I do – if I do. Kisses are important and private between two people who love each other. I don't feel right taking one from you until I feel like at least one of us loves the other."

I smiled. "You are quite noble. I do not care what your birth certificate says."

"Time's up!" yelled Ella.

Henry kissed me on the cheek before standing up and leaving the maze.

Prince Ilya of Northern Europia

"Crown Princess Miriam, it is good to see you again." Prince Ilya greeted me very formally, which threw me off. The previous men who had come to me had been fairly relaxed, albeit nervous, but not Prince Ilya.

"Prince Ilya, you found your way through rather quickly. Please, call me Miriam."

"Ilya," he simply responded as he slowly strolled over to me, exuding confidence and testosterone.

"Will you sit next to me, Ilya?"

He nodded and sat next to me, his icy blue eyes never leaving mine. "I find this custom – interesting."

"This custom? The King's Test in general or this part of it?"

"Both. I must say, I approve. It is wise to make sure someone fitting sits on the throne. Emotions can so often numb the mind to good sense." He began to swing us; I had my legs curled up beneath me and I was facing him. He was facing forward. He was going to be a tough nut to crack. He hadn't even smiled yet.

"How does this part of it make any good sense at all? Even you must see that there is not much you can learn from a single kiss."

He crossed one leg over the other and continued swinging, though he turned to look me in the eyes. "I think we must disagree there, Miriam. You can tell a lot about a person from a kiss."

I laughed. "You sound like my father."

Still no smile. "Good. He is a good King. Have you found him to be a good father?"

My smile faded. Honestly, I couldn't remember my real childhood, but he had been good to me so far in my new life. I looked down to my lap, escaping Ilya's unrelenting gaze. "Yes. Yes, he has been a good father. I trust him implicitly or I would not have allowed this part of the King's Test."

"You do not wish to kiss all those handsome men out there – or me?"

I looked back up and met his stare again. "It is nothing about anyone specific, Ilya. To me, kisses are personal – private." I shrugged and looked back down. "It does not matter what I think about it, though. It is tradition and so, I went along with it."

Ilya stopped swinging and turned his body towards me. His confidence was like some kind of magnet, drawing me a little closer and lifting my head again to look him in the face. He wrapped an arm around my waist and pulled me to him and spoke gently. I bit the corner of my lip, being nervous, not for the first time all day.

"What will your kiss tell me about you, Miriam? Hmm? I know you are resilient because you have been through so much. I know you are beautiful and genuine. What more can I learn from your kiss?

"What will you learn of me? I cannot say what you have learned so far, but hopefully you will learn something of me. Though I understand the validity of this part of the King's Test, I, too, consider a kiss private and personal. And I will have you know, I do not part with them easily. Any other kiss you receive from me in the future must be earned. Yes?"

I was breathless. "Yes. And the same goes for you."

Still no smile.

What is with these men? Why do they all have to be so blooming handsome and confident?

After I replied, Ilya kissed me with commanding passion. He held me tightly against his chest and groaned as he deepened the kiss by parting his lips. Accepting his lead, I followed his mouth's movements. He didn't end the kiss abruptly, but gradually smoothed the kiss out into something soft and sweet.

When he was finished, he asked, "Well, did you learn anything?"

"Yes," I said and swallowed hard. "Did you?"

"Time's up!" yelled Ella.

Ilya finally smiled at me, nibbled at my ear, and whispered, "Absolutely." Separating from me, he kissed me on the cheek and left.

Jonathan Stone of Cedar

When Jonathan strode in, I was star struck for a moment before remembering that there was no way he was the actor who played Thor. Jonathan's cousin, Saul, looked like him, too, but with Jonathan's long hair, he was a spitting image. I swear, he must have been a descendant. He was massive, though not as big as Ilya.

One big difference between the two giants that I noticed immediately was their demeanor. While Ilya was serious, Jonathan had a smile that matched the size of his stature.

"Crown Princess Miriam! Hello!"

Without waiting, he came right over and sat next to me gripping my hand in his and giving it a kiss. By this point, the direct contact from each gentleman was no longer making me anxious, and my hands remained nice and dry when Jonathan took one of them.

"Hello, Jonathan. You can call me Miriam."

"Alright, Miriam. Call me John."

"How are you enjoying Evergreen Palace, John?

"It is beautiful. I do not know if I can go back to living as a commoner after this."

"Surely, it is not *that* bad out there?" I asked, honestly not knowing.

"No! No! That is not what I meant. Even if we were *not* getting compensated for being here, going home would be just fine. Not that I do not want to be here or to be with you. I just –"

I laughed and interrupted him. "It is alright. I understand what you mean."

He smiled and laughed lightly. "You have a great laugh."

"Really? I have always been a little embarrassed of it."

"Yes, really. It is so sweet and airy. It makes me smile just thinking of it."

My legs were still curled underneath me, but unlike Ilya, John had sat with his back against the arm of the sofa with a leg bent and the other dangling. He extended a hand and I took it.

For a moment he just stroked the top of my hand with his thumb. Then, in one swift movement, he pulled me over to himself and kissed me. Just one passionate kiss. After, he spun me around and held me with my back against him.

"Well?" he asked.

Still stunned by the abruptness of the kiss, I asked. "Well, what?"

"Was that alright? I have been nervous all day. I did not want anything too long, so it was inappropriate. But I did not want anything too short, so it would seem I was not interested in you. Because I *am* interested in you. I do not want you thinking –"

I turned so I was facing him and placed my index finger over his mouth and smiled. "You seem to speak a lot when you are nervous, John. *I* think that you over-think things." I gave him a little peck on the cheek. "Your kiss was good. It was nice."

He smiled, kissed me on the cheek and left me before Ella even called for his time to be up. I shook my head at myself, realizing I just assured someone I hardly knew that he was a good kisser.

Prince Joshua of Pacifica

By that point in the day, I was feeling pretty good about the future. So far, all the men had been kind. Alright, well, one had been a bit cuckoo, but he was nice. Ilya had been confident and unsmiling, but not arrogant or unkind. Harrison was still at the top of my list, though. I could look into his eyes all day long.

"Ahem." I looked down from watching the rain hitting the roof again to see Prince Joshua standing there. With his tanned skin and sun-bleached hair, he looked a little out of place with the rainy day as his back drop.

"Hello Prince Joshua. Please, sit. And call me Miriam."

"Alright, Miriam. Call me Josh." He said as he quickly made his way over and sat inappropriately close to me. I edged away a little, but he only scooted even closer.

"So," he said in his Pacifican accent. "We are supposed to kiss, right, Miriam?" He kissed a spot on my jaw line.

I cleared my throat. "Um – yes, though I was hoping to talk first. You know – get to know each other." The whole time I spoke, he was kissing his way down my jaw line.

"We will have plenty of time for that, love." He nuzzled my chin up with his nose and kissed my throat with an open mouth and a swish of his tongue.

I gasped. "Josh, I must insist –"

He pulled his head up from my neck and looked into my eyes. "I hate being in the middle of the alphabet. You are already tired of kissing."

I gaped. "I have not been having make-out sessions all morning, Josh. Every other man has conversed with me first."

Josh shrugged. "I do not see why. It is not like you have any say in who stays or goes." His lips met mine in a fierce, possessive kiss and he held me tight through my struggles. He forced his tongue past my pressed lips and groaned. I felt like vomiting.

After what felt like much too long, Ella finally yelled that his time was up. He separated from me and smacked his lips together. "Delicious. Cannot wait until you are mine forever." At that, he up and left.

Prince Leonardo of Swiss-France

When Prince Leonardo walked through the arch, I fought an audible groan of displeasure. He had been extremely arrogant when he introduced himself to me and hadn't even kissed my hand like he was supposed to.

"Crown Princess Miriam, I would like it if you would call me Leon," he said as he entered.

A little surprised that he made the request for informality first, I said, "Alright. Please call me Miriam."

"*Mais Oui*. May I join you on your sofa?"

"Yes. Please do."

I was sitting with my legs in front of me again. When Leon sat, he leaned back and crossed one leg over his other. "Miriam, I would like to explain something to you."

Leaning back, I bent and tucked my legs beneath me. "What is that, Leon?"

"When you were kidnapped, I could not go out with the search party for you."

Curious as to why he couldn't do what two other Princes had done, I asked, "Why not?"

"You see – My father – he did not approve of my coming here in the first place. He expressly forbade me going off on a dangerous mission to find a woman I had only just met. He is a coward, you see. He does not want me getting into anything that is not set in stone."

"I understand."

"You do? Mother said you would be furious."

I smiled. "No. I am not mad. I understand the necessity to do what is asked of you, even if you would rather not."

"Hmm. I have the feeling we are no longer talking about your rescue."

I sighed. "I have no idea what you mean, Leon."

Leon took my hand and kissed it. "Aw. *Chérie*, you do not need to be false with me. I understand you do not want this King's Test."

I turned my head to look at him. "Can you honestly blame me?"

Facing me, he said, "No. I cannot. I hope you believe me when I tell you I hope you find love with whoever wins the King's Test." Leon leaned to me and placed a short, soft kiss on my lips, then bit his bottom one. "Though, I admittedly hope it will be me."

"Time's up!" Ella yelled.

"*Adieu, ma chérie.*"

Prince Liam of Atlantis

I spent the next few minutes thinking about how I could spend the rest of my life being called "*ma chérie*" and I wouldn't even mind – granted, it probably wouldn't be the *best* plan to judge a man based on his accent.

Leon had been an unexpected happy surprise. I couldn't fault him for not coming to my rescue, really. Eight of the ten Princes didn't come and I understood the stress of trying to please one's father. I certainly didn't want to be spending the day the way I was.

"Hello, Princess Miriam."

I looked away from the rose I had just been examining and stood straight to see Prince Liam strolling through the archway.

Atlantis. How exciting. I wish I could ask about how it was found, but that will have to be a question for Doctor Bartholomew. As Crown Princess, that's information I should already know.

"Hello, Prince Liam. Please, call me Miriam."

"Call me Liam."

Liam had his long, dark hair down and I could see his arm muscles bulging beneath his suit jacket. When he sat next to me, his abs flinched and I wondered if he did more than swim to get them.

This guy is ripped.

Liam was leaning back on the sofa swing, but his head turned to me. "Do you swim, Miriam?"

"Of course. Although, there is not very much opportunity here, as I am sure you have been able to tell over the last few months. I *am* sorry for how long you have had to be here."

Liam laughed. "It is not like you planned to be kidnapped and held captive for two months, Miriam."

I laughed as well and relaxed against the back of the sofa.

"Although, it is a shame that such a beautiful palace has no pool."

I laughed. "We hardly have the time for it here, though I suppose if we *did* have a pool, I might do that more than walk through our forest and fields."

"That would be the first thing I would do if I were King."

"Build a pool? Such high aspirations!"

"It is important to my kind to have such a water source available."

My kind? Not "my people" or "in my culture?"

"I must say, though, I have discovered that walking through a cool rain is nearly as refreshing as a cool swim on a hot day."

"I do love going out into the rain, but it is nicer to sit here and see its beauty without getting wet."

"I like being wet. If we were in Atlantis, we would spend most of our time being wet," he said sternly with a frown on his handsome face.

"I – I am sorry if I offended you, Liam. It was not my intention." I looked down.

Liam sighed and lifted my chin with a curled index finger. After pressing his lips into a straight line, he said, "No. I am sorry. I should not have become upset. It is not your fault that you do not know much about my people. We tend to keep to ourselves. Perhaps over the next few weeks, I can teach you some."

I swallowed. "I would like that, Liam."

Rather than kiss me on my lips, he lifted my chin a little higher and tilted my head so he had access to my neck. When his lips parted and his tongue swirled beneath my ear, a shiver ran up the length of my body and I gently tried to push him away to no avail. He pulled me to him and finally captured my mouth with his, as he tenderly stroked the spot on my neck where his lips had been.

Thinking perhaps the neck obsession was a cultural thing, I brought my hand up to his neck and gingerly stroked beneath his ear to try to get him to loosen his grip around my waist. Unfortunately, he groaned and deepened the kiss; that was when I felt it. As he became more passionate, three slits beneath his ears opened and pulsed.

Trying not to show my panic, I slowly lowered my hand to his chest after a few moments and managed to pull away. He let me that time and looked at me with dreamy eyes. "How did you know to do that?" he asked.

I bit the corner of my bottom lip. "Do what?"

Liam pecked my neck again and pulled away. "Touch my gills."

"Time's up!" Ella yelled.

Thank heavens!

He waited for an answer. "I – I did not know. It just seemed like something you would like." The word 'like' went up in pitch as if I was asking a question, but he didn't seem to notice.

Liam picked up my hand and kissed it before staggering out of the maze.

I don't care if it's close-minded. I cannot marry a – a – whatever he is that isn't totally human.

Lucas Flowers of Willow

The next man to walk in was the rock star himself: Lucas Flowers of Willow. True, he wasn't really a rock star, but he did exude the same attitude one might have. His style certainly screamed that he was a musician. Out of all the gentlemen so far, he was the only one to wear jeans. With them, he had on a button-up forest green shirt with an ivory vest.

"Good afternoon, Crown Princess Miriam," Lucas said.

"Good afternoon. Please, call me Miriam."

I am beginning to feel like a broken record.

"Lucas," he said as he joined me on the sofa and tucked his hair behind his ear with his ring-laden hands.

What else would I call you? Good Heavens. Is he an actual rock star with a rock star name that I don't know about?

"Lucas, do you play an instrument, perchance?"

His eyes widened. "How did you guess?"

Stupid question, Miriam. At least now I know he's not a rock star.

I shrugged and smiled. "Lucky."

"I play piano and guitar."

"Do you write your own music?"

"Yes, in fact. I hear you do some music writing as well. You play guitar?"

"Mmm hmm, but I more enjoy singing or dancing."

"Multi-talented!"

I felt my cheeks blush. "Well, maybe we will need to jam together sometime."

"Jam?"

Carp. I didn't even think about using that term.

"Um – make music together. It was a term used in the twenty and twenty-first centuries."

"Oh. 'Jam.' I like that. I might use that from now on."

I laughed. "Do you sing, too?"

"Yes. I am a tenor, but I can hit some baritone notes sometimes."

"Lovely." It was refreshing to talk with another musician. It had been so long, even in my false life.

Unexpectedly, he began singing in a beautiful tenor voice and I felt like a silly college girl the way his voice turned my insides to goo.

Lady love beneath the silver moon
May I join you in your solitude?

Will you dance with me to this tune?
Let me brighten up your mood

Let me love you
Let me hold you
Let me kiss you, love

Lady love beneath the shining stars
May I join you where you are?
Will you kiss me? Will you hold my heart?
Let me love you near, not from afar

Let me love you
Let me hold you
Let me kiss you, love

Your beauty is surpassed by none
To none can your grace compare
My search for perfection is done
I have found a woman so rare

Let me love you
Let me hold you
Let me kiss you, love

By the end of his haunting melody, his face was merely a couple inches from mine. "Did you write that?" I asked in a breath.

Lucas nodded and his nose brushed against mine. Placing a palm on my cheek, he said, "I wrote it for you." As I leaned my head into his palm, he closed the gap between us and kissed me tenderly. I felt like Odysseus being drawn to the siren.

"Time's up!" yelled Ella, much too early for my taste.

Lucas smiled as he ended the kiss. "See you this evening, Miriam." He gave me another peck before walking out. When he was gone, I felt like a spell lifted off me.

Even though most of these men are kind, I wish more of them would choose to abstain from the kiss. I feel really used right now.

Prince Mamoru of Japan

I must have still had a dreamy look on my face from Lucas' song because when Prince Mamoru came in next, he frowned. "Crown Princess Miriam," he said in greeting.

"Prince Mamoru, you can call me Miriam."

His eyes widened. "That would be most improper."

"Oh. Alright."

Though he did not move from where he was, his frown softened and he relaxed his stance. "I am sorry for my childish behavior earlier today. It is not in my normal character to act in such a way."

"That is alright, Prince Mamoru. Childish behavior happens to the best of us." I smiled, but he did not. I cleared my throat nervously.

"I only came through the maze to apologize and let you know I will not participate in this portion of the King's Test."

I chuckled. "I am afraid it is a bit late for that, Prince Mamoru. You have already made it halfway."

"No. I mean to say that I will not be kissing you."

"Alright. You are certainly not the first today to say that. Might I ask your reason?"

"It is improper."

"I quite agree."

"Also, I do not find myself attracted to you in any way."

I blanched. "What?"

"It is nothing personal. I assure you. If we wed, I will help you provide an heir, but I would rather not kiss you until I have to."

"It actually *is* personal. Quite personal. What are you doing here? Do you honestly expect to spend the rest of your life with a woman you find ugly?"

"No. Not ugly. Just not the prettiest." He shrugged. "And yes. Marriage has nothing to do about feelings. I expect that once an heir is provided I will take up a mistress. Of course, you can have a consort, as well."

I gaped at him. "A mistress? Are you serious?"

"Quite."

"Well, that is not all right with me."

Mamoru shrugged. "You do not have to have a consort if you do not want one."

"That is not what I mean! You think it is improper to kiss me today, but it is totally alright for you to have a mistress? That is outrageous!"

"Time's up!" yelled Ella.

"I will see you later, Crown Princess Miriam."

As Prince Mamoru turned on his heel and left, I mentally added him to the list of Princes I would like to see eliminated that evening.

Percival Andrews of Oak

Completely outraged by Mamoru, I paced and fumed.

What a pig! How could he possibly *think I would go for that? He didn't even care that it bothered me. Of course,* he *thinks I have no say in things, so no wonder –*

"Hello, Crown Princess Miriam." Percival interrupted my raging thoughts.

"Oh, hello Percival. You can call me Miriam. I am sorry you found me fuming."

Percival laughed. "My father is Percival. Please call me Perry."

Some of the tension I was holding relaxed at Perry's levity. "Alright, Perry."

"Let me guess. Prince Mamoru told you about his *magnificent* plan of having a mistress if you marry."

"Yes. Oh, but it is alright because he gave me permission to have a consort," I said with a thick layer of sarcasm and an eye roll.

Perry chuckled dryly. "Roots. I cannot believe he actually presented that idea to you."

I shrugged. "I am not. It is no big secret that I have no say in the outcome of this test. However, with an attitude like that, I cannot see him being the top participant."

"We were all pretty angry with him when he stepped forward this morning like that. Acting like he was all high and mighty. He was the one who started it all."

"That does not surprise me, though I was glad *someone* stepped forward." I sighed. "Enough about Prince Mamoru. Tell me about you."

Perry scratched the back of his neck. "About that. I have been doing a lot of thinking and – well – I do not think I am cut out for this."

I furrowed my brow. "Really? Why do you say that?"

"I do not want to be King. It is not you, Miriam. You would be the best part of being King, but I do not think it is fair to the kingdom or to you for me to participate in this test just so I can become your husband. While I think I am great husband material, I do not think I would make a great King."

"Oh. I see."

"I just did not want you to think I was a loser or stupid when I purposefully throw the first test, whenever that is."

I laughed. "You are far from stupid, but thank you for letting me know. It is important that our future King *wants* to be there."

Perry walked over to where I was standing and gave me a peck on the cheek. "See you at dinner, Miriam." Then, he left.

Too bad he doesn't want to be King. He's one of the nice ones.

Prince Phineas of Britainnia

Why did I let Father talk me into this? I feel so degraded and used. I learned all I need to know from these men just by talking with them. My kisses are too precious for this.

After Perry left, I resumed my seat on the sofa swing, curling my legs beneath me. Closing my eyes, I lay my head down on the back of the sofa.

Why do I call him Father, anyway? In my false life, he was always Daddy or Dad. Is that a piece of my real self? I should ask Ella. I hate not knowing who I am.

A tear slid down my cheek. I was so tired of it all. Putting on a show for everyone and pretending to be a competent Crown Princess was exhausting. Always being on edge and alert, I was constantly catching myself from losing it; I almost *had* lost it when I discovered Liam wasn't fully human. That would have been good information to have.

"Crown Princess Miriam – are you crying?"

Great. Prince Phineas, the gothic romance god, has just caught me crying and I'm going to have to explain myself.

"Prince Phineas! No. Just tired. Please, sit with me. Call me Miriam."

Prince Phineas shook his head in disbelief, but joined me anyway, curling one leg beneath himself and swinging us with his other. We just sat like that for a few moments until another tear slid down my cheek. As Prince Phineas wiped the tear with his thumb, he said, "I do not believe you, Miriam. And if you want me to call you Miriam, you call me Phineas."

I gasped as a vision hit me.

A young man who looks very similar to Phineas is having a conversation with me on my holocomm. By his furrowed brow and bent posture, I think he's very angry about something.

Prince George XV. That's right. He's Phineas' older brother.

"The Council already voted 'nay' on foreigners participating in King's Test for this generation and it is not a decision he can make unilaterally. Surely, he has explained this all before?"

"Yes, he has," Prince George said tightly. *"I am sure your Council and King would not want to cause an international incident with this."*

I leaned forward. "With all due respect, Prince George, there were ten foreign princes told they were under consideration *to participate and only four of you have had a problem with the outcome of the vote. The dirty looks you are giving me, and the fact I have never spoken to you before now, tell me that the loss of your chances with me is not the issue. Might I ask why it is so important to you?"*

"Are you alright, Miriam?"

"Yes."

NO! What the heck was that? A memory?

"Yes, I am fine. It has just been a long day and I am ready for it to be over."

"Listen, I hope you are not offended by this, but I have decided not to kiss you today. If I kiss you, I want it to be natural, not something forced by tradition."

"I am not offended; I am relieved. To be honest, I have been dreading today. When I am Queen and have an heir, she will not have to kiss all her suitors. It is absolutely ridiculous."

Phineas chortled. "I agree. I am sure you can learn just as much about someone without it.

I tried not to be distracted, but I couldn't help it. My first memory, I thought, had come to me and I wondered if more would be coming and when.

Hopefully, they won't all come while I'm in the middle of a conversation. That could become an awkward thing.

"You are nothing like my brother said you would be," Phineas interrupted my thoughts.

I smiled. "I am thinking that is probably a good thing. We only really spoke once or twice."

Phineas chuckled. "Yes, well – he was fairly upset about the first King's Test."

"Time's up!" yelled Ella.

"I will see you later, Miriam." Phineas kissed my hand as he stood up and left.

Prince Ramses of Mesopotamian Egypt

A couple of minutes later, Ella appeared in the archway with an exasperated look on her face. I quirked a brow of confusion at her.

"What are you doing here, Ella?"

"Apparently, Prince Ramses has had a change of heart because of your speech this morning. He found you extremely offensive."

"*I* offended *him*? He was the one acting like a child."

Ella nodded. "I know that. Culturally, as a man, to be chastised by a woman is a sign that she has no respect for him."

"Sounds accurate. Now I have even less respect for him. So, he left?"

"Yes. He marched straight up to his room, packed his things, and took off."

"Good riddance." I paused for a moment as I considered telling Ella about my memory. "Ella, did I ever speak with Phineas' older brother?"

"Prince George XV? Well, King George XV, now, I guess. Yes. Why?"

"I think I had a memory of it just now while I was with Phineas."

"What? That's fantastic! That could mean all your memories will return!"

"It very well could," I said a little despondently.

"What's wrong? Aren't you excited?"

"Yes and no. It would definitely help to have all my real memories back."

"But –"

"But I'm afraid of losing my memories of my false life."

"Why would it matter? None of that really happened."

"I know, but I feel like I learned a lot during that time in my life. I had experiences there that I never had here."

"You're worried about forgetting about your family, huh?" Ella came over and sat by me, putting an arm over my shoulder. I lay my head on her lap and she gently stroked my hair.

"I don't want to forget them or anything from that life. It hurts like crazy that I've lost them, but I don't want to forget them."

"Everything will be alright, Rose," Ella crooned. "I'll be there for you no matter what."

"Thanks, Ella. You're a real gem." I sat up and looked at her in the eyes. "There is something, though, that I've been wondering. I thought you might be able to help me understand."

"I'm no doctor, but you can certainly ask," she responded.

"It's the detail. I remember things from the twenty-first century in such detail. Television shows and housing and appliances and colloquialisms. How is it that I know all that?"

Ella rolled her eyes and giggled. "Yes, well, every heir to the Crown becomes a historian, as well. You were fascinated – no obsessed – with the era just before the Daze hit, the early twenty-first century. You would watch shows and movies from that time, look at digitals of old fashion catalogues and magazines, that sort of thing. It doesn't surprise me that is the time you put yourself in."

I laughed a little. "I guess that makes sense. I'm glad there's *some* reason. Isn't it about time for you to go?"

Ella chuckled. "I'll send in the next man."

I sat up and allowed her to stand. "Who is it?"

"Robert Casey of Petrichoria."

"Ugh. He seems like kind of a tool."

"A what?"

I waved her off. "Never mind. Send him in."

Robert Casey of Petrichoria

"Hello, Crown Princess," Robert said seductively as he entered the center of the maze.

Great. At least it took him a long time to get here. Shouldn't have to be with this guy for long.

"Hello, Robert. Please call me Miriam."

"With pleasure, Miriam." He said my name as if it was a sensual word. I inwardly groaned.

Robert strolled over to me, hands in the pockets of his designer suit. Between his clothing, plucked brows, and well-coiffed black hair, I could see Robert was essentially made of money – and had the stereotypical attitude to go with it. Forget becoming King of Arboria, he was already King of his own little world.

As he sat next to me and put his arm over my shoulders, I shifted so I was sitting a little straighter with one leg crossed over the other. I could hear the gears of his mind turning, trying to figure out the best line to use on me.

"You are more beautiful than all the roses of this garden, Miriam."

That's the best you can do?

"Thank you, Robert. That is very kind of you to say."

Robert leaned over and brushed his lips against my ear lobe. "You are more beautiful than any other woman I have ever known." He kissed my neck and I instinctively pressed my shoulder against my ear.

"Time's up!" yelled Ella.

Robert didn't leave; he quickly turned my head so I was facing him and kissed me. Unsurprisingly, I could tell he had plenty of experience; he was a good kisser. Unfortunately for him, being a good kisser wasn't enough for me to want to keep him.

"See you later, Miriam," Robert said as he abruptly stood and walked out.

Yup. He is *a tool.*

Samuel Harper of Maple

Samuel made it through the maze in record time and I couldn't help but think that Peter and Ella had told him how to get through. He walked straight over and sat next to me. I moved my legs beneath me and examined this man who didn't even say anything when he made it to me.

Clearly, he was nervous. Even though he sat near me, he wasn't even looking at me. I followed his gaze to see what he was looking at only to discover he was probably not looking at anything at all. The poor guy was so anxious, he seemed to have gone to his happy place.

I cleared my throat and he shook himself out of it to finally look at me. "There is no need to be nervous, Samuel. I do not bite. You can even just call me Miriam if it helps."

He chuckled. "Is it *that* obvious?"

I smiled. "Kind of. It is alright, though. I am sure Peter and Ella, as much as they think they are helping, have probably made you more nervous than necessary."

"They are definitely fountains of information."

I shrugged. "They mean well, but can be a little overwhelming sometimes. How do you know them?"

"I have worked in their household as Steward for the last several years. I think it is probably part of the reason I was elected. Duke Peter and Duchess Ella – Elleouise are the favorites among the Nobles of our kingdom."

I smirked at his quick correction to Ella's formal name. "That does not surprise me at all."

"Is it true that your family and friends do not call you Miriam, but Rose?"

"Yes, that is true. My husband probably will, too. We shall see, though."

Samuel cleared his throat. "Um – so – how does this kissing thing work?"

"Generally, two people press their lips together," I joked.

He laughed. "So – I – uh – just do it?"

"Mmm hmm."

He moved so he was facing me and brought his trembling hand up to cup my cheek. "I cannot believe I am about to kiss you. I have heard so much about you over the years and feel a little like I know you already."

I smiled and scooted a little closer to him to ease his nerves and he brought his other hand around my waist. He let out a little breathy chuckle and leaned his face to mine. We closed our eyes simultaneously and he pressed his lips softly against mine, pulling away shortly after. We both bit our bottom lips and laughed.

"That was nice," I said honestly. Samuel seemed like a good man. He could have done as others did and have a make-out session, but he showed me great respect in his restraint.

"Yeah?" he asked.

"Yes."

"Time's up!" Ella yelled.

Samuel released me and stood. Before he left, though, he bent low and gave me another smiling peck.

Chapter 7

Since Saul and Troy didn't make it through the maze, I ended up sleeping on the sofa. It had been an exhausting day and I felt terrible. Not that I was sick, I felt used – tarnished. It shocked me that in this future, a Princess could be passed around twenty men and no one blinked at it.

Finally, Ella came to get me. She gently patted my arm to wake me up. "All done, Rose. It's time to go meet with Uncle Aaron."

Extending my arms and legs into a long stretch, I mumbled, "Alright. Let's get this done."

As we made our way to Father's office, I pumped myself up. I was not going to let them choose for me. After the day I had, I was not about to place my future in anyone's hands, no matter how much I trusted them.

Without ringing the door chime, we let ourselves into Father's office. Peter was already seated on a sofa next to Father. Both were holding cups of coffee and looked at Ella and I like we were about to have a conversation about the weather. Ella took a seat in a chair next to Peter, but I stayed standing.

Crossing my arms, I said, "We need to talk about this."

Father nodded. "Of course. That's why you are here, dear."

"No. You don't understand. I have never felt so demeaned in my entire life. When I am Queen, this tradition is going out the door. I learned everything I needed to know just by talking to the men. The kisses were superfluous."

Father raised a brow. "Alright then. When you are Queen, you can do what you want. Now, let's hear about each man. Let's start with Alan Daniels of Alder."

"No."

"You didn't like him?"

"No. I mean we're not discussing it. I mean *you* are not going to choose who leaves. I mean *I* am going to give you a list of men to send home and you are going to do it."

"That's not how it works, Rose," Peter said with a frown.

I turned my heated gaze on Peter. "I don't care how it is supposed to work, Peter! I have this one chance to be rid of the men who will never love me and I will be pulled out by the roots if I let anyone but myself decide on this."

"I agree with Rose," Ella said.

"Thank you, Ella," I said.

Father sighed with an expression of defeat, "Very well, but you will give reasons for each man."

"Agreed," I said. "Alan Daniels of Alder."

"What's wrong with Alan? He seems like a decent person," Father said.

"He's very nice and sweet. However, he believes that trees are people and regularly converses with them. As King, he wants to make sure everyone accepts and practices his belief. Also, his kiss tasted like tree, so I think he may be eating the one in his room."

Peter laughed hysterically and I couldn't help but smile with him – it *was* ridiculous.

"Alright. Alan Daniels. Gone. Who next?"

"Prince Joshua of Pacifica. He came in and immediately began kissing me. When I asked why he wasn't going to talk to me at all, he said he didn't see why he should, since I have no say in who becomes King anyway."

"Prince Joshua," Father mumbled with gritted teeth as he wrote it down on his Note-Taker.

"Prince Liam of Atlantis. It would have been *magnificent* for someone to tell me he isn't even human!"

"He's human, just different," Peter pointed out.

"He has gills!"

"So? He's hot," Ella said and Peter shot her a look. "What? I mean for Rose. You know – if that is something she is – yeah –"

"Right," said Peter with a pout.

"No. Just – no. I will *not* marry a man with gills. I can't do it. I don't care if it makes me close-minded. Besides, he would never be happy here. There isn't a good warm water source for him to swim in."

"Fine. Prince Liam," said Father.

"Prince Mamoru of Japan. He informed me that while he didn't find me beautiful, he would produce an heir, then take on a mistress." The jaws of all three of them dropped to the floor and Father cleared his throat.

"Prince Mamoru. Definitely gone."

"Percival Andrews of Oak. Decided he doesn't want to be King after all."

"Percival Andrews," Father repeated.

"Robert Casey of Petrichoria. He thinks he's all that and a bag of chips."

"What?" All three asked.

"He is King of his own little world and believes he's God's gift to women. I can't trust that he would be loyal to me."

"Robert Casey. Gone," Father said.

"Prince Estevan of Amazonia, Saul Stone of Birch, and Troy Gold of Juniper. All three couldn't make it through a simple maze."

"I agree. That disqualifies them as far as I'm concerned. And with Prince Ramses of Mesopotamian Egypt leaving, that makes ten. Five of each." Father sighed. "Alright. I think as long as all three of us agree on this list, it will meet the Council's requirement for us to decide."

"Thank you, Father. I need to tell you something else. I – uh – I think I had a memory today of a conversation I had with Prince George XV."

Father jumped out of his seat and wrapped his arms around me. "That's great, Rose! Hopefully that means more will come."

I forced a smile. There was no way I would burst his bubble of happiness about it. I couldn't blame him for being excited. If I was in his place, I would have been. Of course, I was glad to get my memories back, but, as I had told Ella, I didn't want to lose the memories from my false life.

"I'm going to go freshen up real quick for dinner. I know it will make me a little late, but I need a break from people for a few minutes."

"Alright. You go do that, Rose. Let's just keep this between us for now. No need getting your mother's hopes up," Father said.

Though he was being cautious with Mother, there were undertones of excitement as he spoke.

"Oh, Rose! Before you leave, I wanted to let you know that Peter, Thomas, and I need to go home this evening after dinner to take care of a few things, but I will be back tomorrow," Ella informed me.

I nodded and left Father's office without another word to anyone.

Chapter 8

When I walked into the Dining Hall, I was glad I had taken a few minutes to myself. The men were mixed together this time, which satisfied my desire for them to not separate themselves by class. I must have gotten my message through that morning.

Noticing that Frank was seated next to my empty chair, I was even gladder for my time alone. Father must have decided it was only fair since he hadn't seen me at all. As I approached, Frank gave me the stupid grin he had always given me while I was his captive and it sent a shiver up my spine.

"Good evening, Miriam," Frank said as he stood and pulled out my chair for me.

"Hello, Frank," I responded and graciously took my seat.

After taking his seat, he took my hand and kissed it. Leaning over to me, he said, "Long day?"

I whispered back, "You have no idea."

He laughed and released my hand. Dinner was a pleasant affair. Everyone was laughing and talking about their lives. I smiled as I ate in silence, listening in and taking comfort that it was possible for people to get along with each other.

Harrison sat across from me and it was impossible to not take him in. When he smiled, dimples creased his cheeks and his eyes almost closed. His voice was a rich tenor and I could envision him whispering sweet nothings in my ear. Any time I had a thought like that, his gaze met mine and he gave me a knowing smile – as if he knew where my thoughts were – and I was sure my face turned the color of the roses decorating the table.

After dinner, Father stood to make his announcement. "Gentlemen, Ladies. I met with Crown Princess Miriam after your interviews and it sounds like she had a long day. Some of you were perfect gentlemen while others were not. I assume that those of you who were not gentlemen figured it did not matter because she had no say in whether or not you stayed or left."

At that statement, I saw several faces blanch and others smirk.

"Princess Miriam made her recommendations, which have been considered by a committee and myself. The following ten gentlemen will be leaving tonight. When I call your name, please stand and peacefully pack your bags. I will assume you know why you are leaving, but if you do not, you may contact me personally tomorrow morning for an explanation."

All the men looked at Father with intense stares, even those who had previously been smirking. Frank was actually so nervous, he was shaking. I knew I was going to have to find some way to explain to him why he wasn't sent home. Despite the fact that I had forgiven him, he knew that he wasn't my favorite person and I would rather he not be there.

"Alan Daniels of Alder," Father said. Alan furrowed his brow and scratched the back of his neck as he stood and left. The rest of the men exchanged confused glances.

Nice guy. Weird tastes – literally.

"Prince Estevan of Amazonia," Father continued. Prince Estevan stood, nodding his head in understanding and I noticed him looking at Saul and Troy on his way out.

"Prince Joshua of Pacifica," Father said. Joshua stood, pursing his lips. Before leaving, though, he bent over and whispered an apology for his behavior. I nodded in acceptance and he walked out the door.

"Prince Liam of Atlantis," Father said. Liam's face displayed his befuddlement as he stood and left. The Arborians had noticeably began getting more and more comfortable as names were read. Only one of the four names called so far was Arborian and they didn't know that there was going to be five of each.

"Prince Mamoru of Japan." Mamoru shot out of his chair and stomped out the door. No one was surprised by his exit and I even heard several people sigh in relief.

"Percival Andrews of Oak," Father said. Perry stood and walked over to me to whisper a word of gratitude in my ear, then left.

"Robert Casey of Petrichoria," Father said. Robert's jaw dropped at the sound of his name and he didn't move.

"Pardon?" Robert asked.

Father gave him a look. "You are to go pack your bags and leave the palace. We will take care of your transportation."

"I think there has been a misunderstanding. Surely, you cannot be sending *me* home, but keeping a *farmer*!" Robert finally got out of his seat, but walked quickly toward me. "Did *you* request I leave, Miriam?"

I didn't meet his gaze, but said, "It is time for you to leave now, Robert. Show some dignity and go."

Robert raised his hand to hit me and Frank jumped up. Though he was much shorter than Robert, he was skilled in combat and had no problem punching Robert straight in the jaw that he had dropped only moments before. "Your Crown Princess has asked you to leave. Go before things get uglier for you."

"Traitor," Robert muttered under his breath as he left, rubbing his jaw.

Frank straightened his jacket and took his seat amongst the whispered words surrounding him. Surprisingly, Harrison bent over and thanked him, but all I could do is sit there dumbstruck at what had just happened.

Father cleared his throat and continued as if nothing had happened. "Saul Stone of Birch." Saul stood as if he had been expecting his name to be called and left.

"Finally, Troy Gold of Juniper," Father said. Troy stood with the same posture of defeat and left the room. After Troy was gone, Father sat and gestured for me to say something.

"Gentlemen," I began, "you are still here because I see promise in you not only to become King of Arboria, but to become my husband. You each showed me respect and care in one way or another and I really appreciate it. I will have each of you know, however, that while kisses were a part of today, there is no guarantee you will receive any more from me. My kisses from hereon in, will be given of my own free will.

"It has been a long day, so I will be taking my leave now. Have a good evening. I will see you tomorrow."

As I began ascending the steps, I heard talking start up in the Dining Hall. The men were all congratulating each other cordially and I could hear Peter and Ella saying they were going to get Thomas from the nanny and head home. I didn't stop. There was nothing left in me to give; not even another goodbye.

Before I made it to my room, Frank interrupted me, as I thought he would. He leaned over to grab my hand, but a glare from Earl, my new night Guard, enticed him to straighten his posture. "I – uh – I am surprised I am still here."

Stopping at the top of the Core, I turned to look at him. "It would not be very fair of me to ask you to leave when you were not even permitted to take part in the first test."

"Huh." Frank considered that for a moment. "The Council wouldn't let you send me home, would they?"

I pursed my lips. "Nope."

Frank laughed and I rolled my eyes. "How does that feel?" he jeered.

"Shut up, Frank." I turned around to go to my room and Frank held my hand.

"Wait, wait. I'm sorry. I didn't mean to rub it in. I guess I should be grateful to the Council, then. Not you?"

"That would be a correct assessment, yes."

"Is this how it's going to be with us now, Rose?"

I was taken aback by his audacity to use my nickname. "Miriam."

Frank sighed. "Miriam – I guess so."

"Honestly, what did you expect, Frank?"

He shrugged and rubbed his thumb on my hand absentmindedly. "I don't know. You *said* you forgave me."

Gently, I took my hand back. "And I did. I forgave you and didn't send you to the guillotine. You're welcome."

"I don't think anyone uses a guillotine anymore."

"You know very well what I mean." Frank looked hurt. "Listen, I don't want you getting the wrong idea at all, Frank. I don't *hate* you, but I will never, ever love you either. I don't think I can ever forget what you did to me."

Frank swallowed hard and nodded. "I understand, but – what if I win?"

"What *if* you win?"

"Will you spend the rest of your life not hating me, but not loving me?"

"I don't know, Frank. I honestly don't know."

Without another word from either of us, I continued onto my room with Earl following me at a good distance. He was older than Frank and Louis, which I actually requested. I wanted someone who had been in the service for a good amount of time so we were sure it would be someone we could trust.

I patted him on the shoulder as I walked into my room and greeted Adele, who was busy reading *The Lord of the Rings* under my recommendation. "Good evening, Miriam. How was your day?"

"Do not ask. Just get me out of this corset."

Adele laughed. "Alright." She moved behind me, unzipped the dress, then began unhitching the corset. "Steward told me you were on your way, so your bath water is reheating right now."

"Excellent. I could use a hot bath right now." I rolled my head in circles.

As Adele quickly finished with the corset, everything fell and I padded my way to the rose-scented tub. I laid my head back and heard Adele humming something as she picked me out some warm night clothes.

Feeling tired, I closed my eyes to focus on breathing in the steam from my bathwater.

The Man of Night stands over Ella and Thomas' tombstones and laughs maniacally.

"It'sssss time," he says.

I gasped and shot open my eyes. My whole body jolted and water splashed everywhere.

Adele rushed in. "Is everything alright, Miriam?"

"No!" I scrambled out of the tub and ran out of my bathroom. "I don't have time to get dressed. I need a robe now."

"I do not understand. Why –"

BOOM!

A huge explosion interrupted whatever it was she was saying and shook the whole palace.

Still stark naked, I fell to the floor as a wave of memories hit me. All of a sudden, I could remember Ella and our entire history together. I could remember being children and playing in the field of wildflowers behind the palace. I could remember a boy named Stephan, Ella, and I looking at books in the library. I could remember dancing with Peter and watching Stephan and Ella together and thinking what a fine couple they would make. I remembered it all.

"No," I whispered. "Robe! Now!" I demanded.

"Robe. Now." Adele repeated and handed me the nearest robe in the closet. Tying the rope around my waist, I pushed the button to slide open the door and raced out of my room down to the entrance.

"Crown Princess! Wait! It is dangerous!" I could hear Earl yelling behind me, but I didn't care.

No. No, no, no. Please not Ella.

I stepped out of the double doors at the front of the palace to see Ella's hover in flames and Peter face down on the palace steps, his back on fire. Not even thinking about modesty, I threw off my robe and began smacking it on him to put out the flames. When Earl saw me, he threw his uniform jacket over my slender body.

"Get help! Get Doctor Quincy or someone! Quick!" I screamed, panicked. When the flames were out, I bent over to Peter's ear and spoke to him. "It's alright. It's going to be ok. I'm here."

"Rose?" he croaked and looked at my face. His face wasn't burned, so I placed my palm on his cheek.

"I'm here, Peter. It's alright."

"Ella. Thomas." His face scrunched up and he began sobbing. "I'm sorry."

"No. None of that. We both thought the danger had passed. We will be here for each other. Yeah?"

Through his tears, I heard him saying something about how everyone he has ever loved has now been lost to him. All I could do was keep my hand on his cheek and coo words of encouragement at him. I felt a blanket get put over me and looked up to see Phineas. "Thank you," I said to him and noticed all ten men left were now outside and watching.

Sirens blared as the fire hover came to put out the fires and the ambulance arrived to transfer a screaming Peter into the back of its vehicle. I started to climb in with him, but was directed away by Doctor Quincy, who had come himself to the call. "There is nothing you can do, Crown Princess."

"I can be there for him," I said.

"Rose," Peter mumbled.

"Please," I begged.

"I am sorry. I cannot bring you with us. I will call you directly when I have an update," Doctor Quincy said.

"At least let me say goodbye," I said. "So he knows I didn't just abandon him."

Doctor Quincy nodded and I climbed in. Placing my palm back on his cheek, I said, "Peter, Doctor Quincy needs me to stay here. I promise, as soon as I can, I will see you."

"Rose," Peter said my name like a prayer.

"I'm sorry, Peter."

Peter took my hand and kissed it, then released me. Harrison was standing at the ambulance exit and helped me out. He folded me into his arms and I cried as the ambulance took off. Pretty soon I had ten men surrounding me in one big hug, all telling me it would be alright and they were there for me.

I wasn't so sure that everything would be alright. My memories of Ella returned when she died. If that was the way I was going to be getting my memory back, I didn't know if I wanted it after all.

Chapter 9

After a good long cry, I went back up the Core with my entourage of men behind me. Father had refused my half-hearted offer to stay behind with him to answer questions from the Petrichorian City Guard. Because he was dealing with enough, I did not tell him about my sudden memory emergence.

Ella was such an intricate part of my life, that I remembered some other things, too. For example, she had been there shortly before I went into the freeze when the Council unanimously voted for Peter and me to be married. I knew Peter and I had been together, but I didn't realize we had been engaged.

Not that it mattered anyway. He was now *way* past the age qualifications and the King's Test had already begun.

When I made it to my room, I was still in my head, so when I turned around to thank everyone, I was surprised to only see Earl standing there. He noticed my confused expression, then explained that the men split off when they got to their floors. I lowered my head and nodded as he wished me a good night and finally put on the satin nightgown Adele had laid out for me. The sleeves were loose and long and it felt like a soft hug.

Just as I was getting in bed, someone knocked at my door. As I made my way to my door, I heard Earl chastising the knocker, then a man with a southern accent telling him off. I smiled as I realized

Harrison had come to see me. I pushed the button to slide the door open.

"Your Crownship, I am sorry, but I could not stop the gentleman from knocking."

Harrison smiled like a cat who caught a bird. "He blocked the chime, so I had to go with old-fashioned knocking."

Earl frowned at him, but I just laughed dryly. "It is quite alright, Earl. Prince Harrison is welcome any time."

Earl bowed and begrudgingly stepped out of the way so Harrison could come in. Harrison straightened his posture and made a show of walking regally into my room. I shook my head and smiled at the floor. When the door slid closed behind me, Harrison swooped me up in his arms and held me. Feet dangling beneath me, I breathed him in and sighed into his chest.

Setting me down, Harrison tilted my head up to face him and cupped my face in his big hands. "I'm sorry to disturb you. I know you probably just want to go to bed, but I had to see you to make sure you were alright."

"Thank you. I'm not." I began crying again and he pulled me to him.

"That's what I thought." Harrison stroked my hair and placed his cheek on top of my head. "You just cry what you need. I'll be here for you."

"You always seem to be," I sobbed. After a few minutes, I sniffled and looked up at him, meeting his Kona-blue eyes. "Why, Harrison? Why have you cared so much? You came to rescue me. You were gentle with me today in the garden. You waited for me outside the ambulance. You are here now. You know I have no say in who will be my husband, so why have you showed me such concern?"

"Oh, Miriam." He wiped my tears away. "Can't you feel it?"

"Feel what?"

"Destiny unfolding before us. Every time we touch, I feel complete. Cacti, I sound like a woman right now, but I can't help it with you. You already feel like a part of me. How could I not concern myself with you?"

"Please tell me that you are not taking advantage of me when I am weak."

"I'm not. I wouldn't. Look." Harrison sighed. "I will tell you something, alright? Something I have never told anyone."

"Are you sure it is something you want to tell me?"

"Absolutely, because it will explain how I know certain – things about you. Maybe it will help you feel more relaxed; more like you can trust me."

"I trust you."

"Not completely, but that's understandable."

Does he know about my memory problem?

Harrison chuckled as if he could hear my thoughts. "Sorry. I don't do it on purpose."

My eyes widened. "Do what on purpose?"

"I can – this is going to sound crazy."

"Try me."

"Now, don't be mad. I did not learn what I know on purpose. My mama taught me better than that. I can – you see –" He tightened his lips and gave me a curt nod as if he had just made a big decision. "I can read people's minds. I have gotten pretty good at controlling it, but with some people, their thoughts seep in anyway. Those people are usually my close friends and family – loved ones."

"Oh my goodness." I stepped out of his embrace and he let me. "What do you know?"

"I know you don't remember anything from before your cryogenic freeze."

I sat down on the edge of my bed.

"I do not know how you do it. How you live every day like nothing is wrong. You are a remarkable woman, Miriam."

Looking at him again, I was sure my face was so pale it was nearly translucent. Harrison came over on his knees and took my hands.

"What do you want?" I asked, sure that anyone with the information would try some kind of blackmail on me.

"What? Nothing, Miriam. I am just trying to tell you that you don't need to be alone here." He kissed my knuckles. "I saw your memories of Ella rush back to you during the explosion. I heard your worried thoughts for Peter. Please, you can open up to me."

I can't believe it.

"Believe it," he said with a smirk.

"How?" I asked.

He shrugged. "I don't know. Just like you don't know where your visions come from."

Suddenly, the fact that he had David's eyes made total sense to me. He could *see* me the way David could. He could truly *know* me in a way no one else could.

"Should I be flattered that I remind you of your late husband?"

Completely embarrassed, I let go of his hands and brought mine up to cover my face. "Trees and blossoms. How embarrassing."

92

"Don't be embarrassed. I think it's sweet and another sign. Can't you see, Miriam? We are meant to be. Destiny unfolding."

At that point, I couldn't disagree with him. Destiny. Fate. Whatever one would call it. It was becoming clearer by the day that my false life was laden with subtle visions as well. David looking like Peter. Frank being a cop I couldn't trust. Ella being there for me in both versions of my life. Tom and Thomas being and looking so similar. Now, the similarities between David and Harrison's eyes.

I met his blue gaze and put my hand to his cheek. "As much as I would love destiny to have its way, it will be the King's Test that decides for us."

"I will win. I know it." With that confident assertion, he put my hands around his neck and pulled me flush against him with a kiss. A passionate kiss. He was right; his kisses felt more right than they had with anyone else besides David. Our mouths even moved to the familiar rhythm David's and mine used to. Our tongues touched the same way. Our hands gripped each other the same way. When he separated from me, I still had my eyes closed. "We are right, Miriam. This feels right," he whispered into my ear as he stood up. "You know where I am if you need me. I will let you get some sleep now." He turned and began walking to the door.

Yeah right. Like I'll be getting any sleep tonight.

He looked over his shoulder and grinned stupidly at me.

"That's not fair," I said and his smile grew bigger.

Chapter 10

Ella and I are teenagers laying in a patch of flowers and grass we found in the forest. We hold hands. While I am awake, watching the breeze in the trees, Ella has fallen asleep.

"Hey, Ella?" I ask.

Ella snorts and shoots straight up. Laughing, I grab my stomach and roll a bit. She glares at me. "This better be good."

I shrug. "Probably not, but it was worth it." I laugh a little harder and she nudges me with her knee before lowering herself again.

"What do you think of Count Peter?" I ask.

"Count Peter of Juniper?" She answers my question with a question.

"Yes. Do you know any other Count Peter?"

"No. I don't know. He's good looking and you two seemed to have fun at the ball last night."

I sigh. "He's one of the participants, you know."

"Everyone knows who all the participants are, Rose."

There's a comfortable silence that falls between us, but I'm not done talking yet.

"It's not fair," I say.

"No. It isn't," Ella responds

"I'm glad you understand me, Ella. I don't feel like anyone else does."

"I'll always be here for you, Rose. You know that, right?"

I turn and look at her face. "Will you be my Crown Princess' Maiden?"

Ella turns her head sharply to me. "Really?"

I laugh. "Yes, really. Who else would I choose? You're my best friend, Ella."

Tears well up in Ella's eyes. "I would be honored to be your Crown Princess' Maiden someday, Rose."

I woke up from the dream totally drenched in sweat with Adele hovering over me. "Did you have another dream, Miriam?" Adele asked. I nodded and she helped me sit up. "Was it about Ella?" I nodded again, not revealing that it wasn't just a dream, but a memory.

"It will get easier, Miriam. Not right away, but it will," Adele assured me.

No. It won't.

I glanced out the window and saw the dim green light of the Space Needle. "What time is it, Adele?"

"6:00 AM."

"Why am I awake right now?"

"Emergency meeting of the Arborian Council."

"Ugh," I grunted as I started to lower myself back into bed.

"Oh, no, Crown Princess. You need to get up. I will start your shower for you. You stink."

I lifted a hand up in a dismissive wave as she went into the bathroom. "Gee. Thanks, Adele."

A slap on my door caused me to jump out of bed. "I am sorry, Your Highness, but the Crown Princess is getting ready for a special session of the Arborian Council."

"Now, listen here, Earl, is it? Yes, Earl. Miriam will not mind seeing me if she is awake." Harrison was trying to reason with Earl.

Adele peeked around the door frame. "What is one of the King's Test participants doing here so early in the morning?"

"Being nosy," I muttered as I padded to the door to open it.

When I did, Harrison gave a smug grin to Earl and started to come in. I extended my arm to block the doorway. "Earl, can you give us a moment, please?"

This time, Earl gave Harrison a smug grin and walked away. "Your night Guard has attitude. I like your day Guard better," Harrison said. He was completely disheveled. His hair was standing up, flat on one side and he was wearing red pajama bottoms with a white tank.

"What is it, Harrison?" I asked with a gravelly voice.

"I like your voice in the morning," he said dreamily.

"Harrison," I began, pinching the bridge of my nose. "Thank you for your compliments first thing in the morning. But please get to your point. I just found out I have an emergency session of the Arborian Council to get ready for."

"Oh. That's what it was about."

"What?"

Harrison tapped his head. I rolled my eyes and whispered, "What did you hear?"

"'No, it won't.' Are you alright?"

I sighed and looked behind me at Adele, who was suddenly very interested in one of my trees. I leaned forward with a tilted head and quietly told him, "Adele was just telling me it will be alright after I had a dream and woke up drenched in sweat."

"I noticed."

I tipped my head to the side in an annoyed gesture. "Thanks, Harrison."

"Was it a dream or a vision?" Harrison whispered.

"Neither. It was a memory. Of Ella." I looked at my feet and tapped my toe on the floor.

Feeling him stroke my arm, I met his eyes. Harrison said, "You know, it will get easier. You won't ever forget her, but life will get easier."

"Thank you, Harrison, but you can't come every time you accidentally hear my thoughts," I whispered.

He took my hand and kissed it. "That is not fair. I cannot stay away knowing you are sad."

I smiled. "But people will wonder how you always know, Harrison. I do not want you in danger."

"Alright. I won't come *every* time, but I won't promise I will never come."

"Sounds good. Now. I need to get ready. No eavesdropping on the Council session, alright?"

"I will do my best." Harrison kissed me on the cheek before leaving. "Earl, my man! You can come back now!" He jovially shouted as he walked back to the Core.

Pushing the button to slide the door shut, I shook my head and turned to Adele. She had a cheshire grin on her face. "Do not," I said as I padded over to the bathroom.

Her smile got impossibly bigger. "What?"

"Do not say a word." I drew my nightgown over my head.

"I like his accent. And he is cute."

"He is *not* cute," I snapped jokingly. "He is hot."

Adele giggled as I closed the bathroom door and hopped in the shower. As I quickly cleaned myself, I shut my eyes and hummed the Rose Waltz.

I wonder if Harrison can hear me if I hum or sing in my mind.

With a smile, I stopped humming out loud and began humming in my mind. When I got out of the shower, I kept on mentally humming. I smiled at Adele when I stepped out of the bathroom and kept on mentally humming. As she dressed me and did my hair and makeup, I kept on mentally humming. Then, I made a mental note to ask Harrison later if he heard it.

I stood in front of the mirror and admired the sleek brown pinstripe suit – with a pencil skirt and no pants, of course – Adele had chosen for me. She walked up behind me and put my Crown Princess tiara on my head, carefully maneuvering it so it didn't disturb my braided chignon.

"How *do* I do it?" Adele asked with a smile.

"You have a perfect canvas," I replied in mock boastfulness and turned to give her a hug. "Thank you, Adele."

She wiped a tear from her eye and cupped my face in her hands. "I always aim to please you, Miriam. I am glad I was able to bring a smile to you." She patted my cheek and left.

With a sigh, I straightened my suit jacket and walked out of my room. I smiled to Louis in greeting and he nodded in return. Sure the emergency session was about the explosion last night, I tried to calm myself. This was a true test as to how prepared I really was to be Crown Princess of Arboria.

How prepared am I? How about not at all? How about, I am still having difficulties remembering our history, much less how to run a kingdom in the future?

As I passed the third floor, Phineas joined me on the steps. "How are you feeling this morning, Miriam?"

I looked at him and quirked my brow to let him know it was a stupid question, then looked forward again.

"Sorry. I suppose that *was* a stupid question."

When we got to the second floor, he grabbed my wrist to stop me from going further down the steps. "I am going to breakfast now, Miriam. Harrison told us about the meeting. If you need anything when you are done, please let me know." He scooped my hand to his lips and kissed it before releasing me and heading to the Dining Hall.

Shaking my head to expel the tension just brought on by Phineas' affections, I continued my trek down the stairs. When I walked into the Council Chamber, chin up and shoulders back, everyone stood and bowed. As I nodded acceptance and took my seat, everyone else followed suit except Father.

"Thank you, everyone for coming all the way to Petrichoria for this emergency session of the Arborian Council. As you are all aware, late last night Duchess Elleouise of Maple and her son, Count

Thomas of Maple, were killed in a hover explosion right outside the front doors of Evergreen Palace."

A choking sob filled the silence and I noticed Peter for the first time, sitting as if he had not been on fire the night before. He covered his mouth and lowered his head.

How? Must be some kind of medical advancement.

Father nodded solemnly to Peter and continued. "Upon initial investigation, it is clear that the explosion was intentional and probably meant for all three Nobles of Maple to be in the hover when it happened. Because of this, I have called the Council together to request a shortening of the King's Test."

My straight face faltered as my left eye twitched a little upon hearing his request.

"Before discussing that, what of Duke Peter?" Delegate Juniper spoke up. Peter lowered his hand from his mouth and shot a confused look at her.

"What about me, Delegate?" he asked.

She cleared her throat. "Well – it is only that Duke Peter is now single and he *was* originally engaged to our Crown Princess. Should we not cancel the test and resume the engagement?"

Peter frowned at her. "Delegate Juniper, I just lost my *wife* and *son* last night and you are suggesting I take another wife so soon?"

"Not only that," Father piped in, "But we cannot cancel the test once it has begun. It is unprecedented and I do not see the need to do it. Not to mention the international repercussions of calling it not. Also, Duke Peter is now beyond the age qualifications for marriage to Crown Princess Miriam."

"I agree with you, Your Majesty, about continuing the King's Test, but surely an exception for age qualifications can be made considering the circumstances," Delegate Birch said.

"I am not sure what you are getting at, Delegate Birch," Delegate Maple said.

"What I am saying is that perhaps we should let the only single nobleman of marrying age participate in the King's Test," Delegate Birch said.

The room fell silent as everyone considered the possibility. Peter was pale and shocked, but clearly not opposed to the idea. Although, he was disgusted with the idea of marrying so soon a moment ago, now he seemed to be thinking it over.

I was horrified at the thought of marrying my best friend's widower, especially since I felt like I was falling in love with Harrison – and especially since Peter had been so arrogant and pushy since I woke from my freeze. Glancing over to Father, I was surprised to see him actually considering the idea himself.

"Perhaps an exception could be made," Father said. I widened my eyes, but said nothing. "If Duke Peter wished to participate and the participant from the Maple Province agreed to allow his place to be taken."

I opened my mouth to say something, but Peter's resigned sigh interrupted me. "I will speak with Samuel," he said.

"What?" I asked and everyone looked at me. "Are we seriously having this discussion right now? Not only has Duke Peter's family been dead for less than half a day, but he is ten years older than me! This is absurd!"

"Crown Princess, surely you can see the dilemma. The only reason we are even having a King's Test at all is because Duke Peter felt he could no longer wait for you. It is only fair that he get his chance," Delegate Maple said.

I looked at Peter. "Is that how you feel? That you deserve a chance? That you are willing to remarry mere months after your family was *killed*?"

Peter looked at his hands with a flush of guilt sweeping over his face. "I do," he said plainly. I pressed my lips into a straight line and said nothing else. I was mortified at his statement to the Council and his unspoken declaration to me that he still loved me and wanted a chance.

"I move to allow Duke Peter the chance to participate in the King's Test if Samuel Harper of Maple is willing to give his place to him," said Delegate Maple with a pointed look at me.

"Seconded," said Delegate Juniper.

"All in favor?" Father asked.

"Aye," said everyone but me.

"All opposed?" Father asked.

"Nay," I said under principle.

"The ayes have it. Duke Peter, Samuel Harper, and I will meet after this session of the Council and discuss the possibility. I will let everyone here know the result of the meeting.

"Now, I will make this simple. There are ten men left in the King's Test. I move that the five tests that were supposed to take place once a week over the next several weeks be pushed up to everyday. At the end of each test, one Arborian and one Prince will go home.

"The final test will be between the final Arborian and the final Prince this Saturday."

"Seconded," said Delegate Juniper.

"Wait!" I interrupted. "Do we not want to discuss this? This is a pretty major change." Now they were talking about the possibility of marrying Peter only weeks after Ella and Thomas were killed.

"No discussion is needed," Delegate Sequoia said. "The Royal family is possibly in danger. We reacted inappropriately the last time and we will not make the same mistake again."

I knew he was talking about before when the Council had been unresponsive and I ended up going into cryogenic freeze. I waved my hand in a defeated gesture to Father to go ahead with the vote.

"All in favor?" Father asked.

"Aye," said everyone, including, with much distaste, me.

"We have a unanimous vote. The King's Test will move forward in the way I described starting today. Crown Princess Miriam, I need you to go change into clothing appropriate for the outdoors after this session is adjourned. Meet the King's Test participants and myself out at the tree line at 4:00."

"Yes, sir," I said and glared at him.

"I now call this emergency meeting of the Arborian Council adjourned. Everyone please be safe on your rides home."

The second Father closed the meeting, I stood from my seat and strode out the door.

"Rose, please, wait!" Peter was calling behind me and rushing to catch up, but I didn't stop. I was mortified with everything that had just happened. He was unable to catch up to me until I had arrived at the second floor, where he grabbed my hand and pulled me off toward the branch that led to the library.

"Let me go! I have to go change and *you* have a meeting to attend!" I said to him with a sneer. I turned as we entered the branch and saw the participants of the King's Test had gathered at the doorway of the Dining Hall. They all looked worried.

Peter pulled harder as I struggled against him. "I said, 'let me go!'" I yelled as he flung me into the Library and locked the door behind us. Thrown off balance, I stumbled onto the floor, ripping my pencil skirt, and crawled away. When I reached the wall, I turned around to see Peter walking slowly toward me.

My breathing and heart rate increased as I had flashbacks of being in captivity with Frank. Bringing my arms up to my face to block Peter from view, I struggled to maintain some semblance of dignity in my composure. I heard him sit next to me and he gently brought my arms down and held my hand.

I looked over to him, wide eyed and terrified and he seemed to finally see that I was scared. Realization dawned on his face at what he had just done. "Oh, Rose." He kissed my hands and turned onto his knees to face me. "Rose, Rose. I'm so sorry. I – I didn't think. I didn't mean to trap you – I mean, I did, but I didn't think about how it would affect you. Please, don't be scared. I am *not* going to hurt you or do anything to you." During his pleading, he had been kissing my hands with his dry lips.

"How – How could you, Peter?" I asked, hoping he would understand my question without making me explain.

"How could I not?" he asked. "I lost my chance with you before and now – it is tragic about Ella and Thomas – Who better to be with than you, who can understand what it is like to lose a lover? Whom I have never stopped loving?"

I looked down at my lap. "Peter, I – I have to tell you – I do not feel the same way about you. I think I am in love with someone else."

"I understand that, but there is a chance you could love me again if I win the King's Test and I am willing to take it." Peter kissed my cheek before standing. "I will prove myself to you if it is the last thing I do." With that, he walked out the door, leaving me alone with my thoughts.

Chapter 11

I sat in the library for a few more minutes, totally baffled at the sudden turn of events. When Peter left, I saw that Louis had followed us and was standing outside the library. He probably knew I wasn't up to seeing anyone and let me have my privacy.

My head was reeling with all the changes I had gone through lately. Beyond waking up two hundred years in the future to a life I couldn't remember, I had been kidnapped, coronated Crown Princess, lost my best friend, and told I would be engaged in less than a week.

Right – and my best friend's widower, who happens to be my ex-fiancé, just declared his love for me and would be participating in a test that could result in him becoming my fiancé again – even though he was now ten years older than me.

How much more messed up can my life become?

Even though I knew Harrison could hear my thoughts a mile away, I couldn't help but think specifically to myself. It kept me from going crazy sometimes. Standing up, I smoothed my torn suit and walked out the door. Louis followed close as I made my way up the Core to my room at the top.

Adele wasn't in my room that time, so I just went into my closet and picked out my own clothes. Missing the presence of denim in my wardrobe, I found some tight brown leather pants, knee high green leather boots, and a green long sleeve shirt that was snug against my skin.

I couldn't remember the material name; it wasn't important. What mattered was that the outfit was what Father had requested; it was fitting for going outside to do whatever it was he had in store. More-than-likely, I wouldn't be doing much, it would be the men doing all the work.

Removing my tiara, I brushed out my braided chignon, then twisted my tresses into a long side braid. Knowing it would be sturdier than the delicate bun Adele had set my hair in earlier, I gave it a quick tug to test it. Gently, I ran my hand down the soft braid to make sure it was tight and wouldn't become frizzy as the day wore on.

Glancing at my clock, I saw it was still before noon. I didn't feel like seeing Father or Peter, so I made the decision to skip lunch. I picked up Adele's copy of *Lord of the Rings* and plopped onto my sofa to read. Unfortunately, I was so tired from the long night and emotionally draining morning, I ended up falling asleep.

The door chime woke me up at around 4:30 and I jumped out of my seat to answer it. I slammed on the button and the door slid open to reveal an unhappy Father on the other side. I pressed my lips into a straight line and straightened my posture, unwilling to admit I was not purposefully late.

"Why are you not at the tree line, Miriam? You are a half hour late," Father said crossly.

"I was feeling overwhelmed and needed a break from everything for a bit," I responded.

"A bit? You have been locked up here since the meeting this morning. Really, I do not know what upset you about it."

"Are you serious, Father? Ella's *widower* is now competing for my hand in marriage less than twenty-four hours after her and her son's death. On top of that, he is *old*. On top of *that*, I am going to be engaged by the end of the week! You tell me how I should be feeling right now!"

Father softened his expression and spoke more kindly to me. "I understand things are tough for you right now and you are feeling overwhelmed. I compacted things for the King's Test because I am concerned for your safety. The Petrichorian City Guard is looking into the explosion further. We have no way of knowing if the threat extends to you."

Not wishing to further the discussion, I bit my lower lip. Not unkindly, I said, "Fine. I am ready. Let's go."

I followed Father down the Core and out to the tree line with my head down. I didn't know what to expect, except that I knew Peter would be there; Samuel seemed the loyal sort and if his Duke wanted to participate, he would give up his spot. I was a little sad he didn't bother saying goodbye, but I didn't blame him either.

When we approached the tree line, the men were standing in a line. Tilting my chin up, I smiled as I stood at attention next to my Father, who had obviously told the men to do the same. True to form, Harrison broke attention by smiling back. Phineas nonchalantly elbowed him and smirked when Harrison jumped a bit.

"Gentlemen, as you are all aware, there was an explosion last night that killed Arboria's Duchess Elleouise of Maple and her son, Count Thomas of Maple. Our local Guard is investigating, but it seems like it was purposeful and that Duke Peter was meant to be included among the dead."

Peter had been trying to make eye contact with me the whole time I had been there so far, but I refused to look at him. He made me sick and I felt it was important that he know it.

"Because Duke Peter is among the original Nobility of Arboria and is not too far outside the age qualifications," I snorted when Father said that and he gave me a dirty look. Clearing his throat, he continued, "Samuel Harper of Maple has graciously given his spot in the King's Test so Duke Peter may participate."

I looked along the line of men and, by the looks of things, many of them were as disgusted with Peter as I was. Although, Frank looked more angry than disgusted. Not that I really cared about what Frank thought.

"Because the explosion seemed to be intentional, an emergency vote of the Arborian Council has resulted with the King's Test now ending Saturday evening rather than five weeks from now."

A few jaws dropped and the brows of all men were furrowed. It was not a popular decision among them. Seeing as how I was not happy with it myself, I was not surprised.

"Today's test involves a variety of activities in the forest. A few months ago, on Crown Princess Miriam's twenty-first birthday, she was kidnapped and held captive for two months. During that time, she showed great courage and resourcefulness in not surrendering, and in making her own way home to us. The tests today are focused on your own courage and resourcefulness."

All the men glared at Frank and he shifted uneasily on his feet. I grinned at his discomfort.

"While we are out in the forest, you will first complete an obstacle course high in the trees. You will climb a cliff face, cross a log connecting two tree tops, then swing on ropes until you make it to the ground, when your time will end. Whoever has the quickest time will get the highest score.

"Next, you will go on a hunt in the forest for a list of items. Whoever returns to the tree line the quickest will get the highest score."

Why do I even need to be here?

Harrison smirked at my thought and I rolled my eyes, slightly irritated that I couldn't even have a thought to myself anymore.

"Your final test will involve finding your way in the dark. Crown Princess Miriam will hide in a predetermined spot deep in the woods and it will be up to you to find her. When she is found, she will give you an item to return with. Whoever finds her and returns the quickest will get the highest score. The final gentleman will bring her back.

"At the end, I will average out your scores. The Prince and Arborian with the lowest scores will be out."

I noticed Lucas, the rock star, kicking the dirt with his toe. He wasn't feeling very certain of himself and I couldn't blame him. Among the men present, he was certainly not the strongest of them and the way his faced turned a bit green when Father was talking about the first activity didn't bode well for him.

Alex looked excited – he always did – and I could see he and Harrison giving each other friendly competitive glances. Henry looked like he had swallowed the sweetest apple in his orchard and John was casually stretching his bulging arms.

Shaking my head with a smile, I said, "Let the tests begin!" and the excited men shouted out. Father and I led the men out into the forest to the cliff side. It was around a mile away, so the men were able to have a little warm up before they got ready to go up.

I looked up the wall of rock and couldn't believe how tall it was. There were plenty of places to hold on to and step and I was mapping out how I would go about ascending the face as if it was me having to do it. I briefly wondered how I knew how to climb the wall. David always tried to get me to go rock climbing with him, but I was always too afraid.

When I looked straight again, the world spun for me. As I staggered about to regain my balance, I felt two strong hands hold on to my arms to help. "You have a beautiful singing voice in your head," Harrison whispered in my ear and I smiled.

Turning around, I gave him an unashamed embrace and reveled in Frank and Peter's glares in our direction. "Thank you, Harrison. I was wondering if you could hear that."

Still holding me, he waggled his eyebrows and whispered, "Were you in the shower?" I pushed him away playfully and he laughed.

"Way to ruin a moment, Harrison," I said as I walked away and he laughed louder.

I made my way over to Lucas, who was looking more and more like he was going to throw up with every passing moment. He eyed the cliff like it was the Reaper who had come to take him away. Placing my hand on his shoulder, I asked, "Are you alright? You don't look like you're feeling well."

Lucas swallowed hard. "It is just – I have a – thing – about heights."

"Oh." I took his hand and gave it a little squeeze to get him to look at me instead of the towering rock wall in front of us. "Look, I loved your song. Truly, it was the most beautiful song I have heard in a long time. But there is more to this than romancing me, unfortunately. Being King means facing your fears head on. I think you can do that." I gave him a wink and he pulled me in for a trembling hug.

"Thank you, Miriam. That means a lot to me. You have no idea. I will do this. I will prove myself to you." He released me and I continued walking toward Father until I felt someone grip my hand and pull me behind a large tree. It was Frank.

"What do you want, Frank?"

"What was that with Prince Harrison?" he demanded as if he had a claim on me.

"That is not an answer to my question. That is another question. Also, whatever is going on between Harrison and me is not something you should concern yourself with," I stated blandly.

Frank tightened his lips. "It is too soon for you to fall for anyone."

I snorted. "Like you have any say in that, Frank – or any room to talk, for that matter. You forget. I am no longer your captive." I tried to take my hand back, but he tightened his grip. "You are hurting me."

"Listen, Miriam. You have to know that choosing someone foreign will be a terrible thing for our kingdom."

"*I* will be choosing no one, Frank. The decision has been completely taken out of my hands." I slapped his hand that was gripping me hard and he withdrew it from me. "As for who I decide to show affection to, it is none of your business. The next time you touch me like that, it will be more than your hand being slapped."

Frank nodded, but glared at me as I rounded the tree and walked over to stand with Father. Harrison was crouching and getting ready to go. I observed the profile of his face. His jaw was set with determination and I was impressed that he was able to stay focused even though I was sure he had sensed everything that had just happened with Frank.

"Ready. Set. Go!" Father said and Harrison shot off, officially beginning the real tests.

Part II

Chapter 12

Harrison moved up the cliff like a gecko. He moved so quickly, I couldn't see his foot or hand placements. When he started walking across the log, he blew me a kiss and winked at me and several men around me groaned at his over-confident gesture. Rather than swing on all the ropes down to the ground, he only did half of them, then flipped off halfway down. He was finished before I could really process any of what he had done. Father took his time, then asked for the next volunteer.

I heard a familiar popping behind me as Frank rolled his neck and stretched his arms. He glared at Harrison. While Harrison and Alex had been friendly in their competition earlier, there was nothing friendly about the way Frank looked at him then. By the expression on Harrison's face, the feeling was mutual.

At Father's "Go," Frank shot off. If Harrison was a gecko, Frank was a spider. He scuttled up the wall and leaped across the log. Only needing two ropes to get down, he landed with a huge thud and thrust his arms in the air. As Ilya readied himself, Frank walked over to me as I leaned against the tree and pressed himself flush against me. The stench of his sweat was overwhelming.

"No one stands a chance. You want to play it this way? I will beat your precious Prince Harrison at every test. If you desire to be a prize, I will make you mine," Frank whispered menacingly in my ear.

I saw a hand with long fingers come down hard on Frank's shoulders and he jumped. "Expertly done, Frank. There are water bottles over there by Prince Alexander." Phineas' voice was laced with warning.

Frank shrugged his hand off and backed away from me after planting a possessive kiss on my cheek. "It is 'Francis,' Prince Phineas," Frank corrected.

As he walked away, I let out the breath I did not realize I had been holding and tried to slow my heartbeat.

"Next!" Father shouted and Alex made his way over to have his go.

Phineas cupped my face in his hands and my lower lip trembled. "Are you alright?" he asked.

"He scares me, Phineas. I do not know what I will do if he – if he –"

"He will not. We will not let him."

I noticed Harrison pacing far over Phineas' shoulder. My emotional state must have been driving him mad, but he was staying away and letting Phineas handle it.

"How? How can you even say that? There is no way to guarantee that."

"*Francis* is physically strong." Phineas said his name like a curse and rubbed my cold arms. "We already knew that, but he is not all that smart. After the mass elimination last night, he is an idiot for cornering you like that."

"Next!" Father shouted and Henry stepped up. I started to feel like I was at the DMV – except people were moving through the line at least a hundred times faster and the scenery was better.

I shrugged and looked down. "He is smart enough to know that I really do not have any more say in the matter. Last night was my only chance." I sniffed. "I did what I could."

Phineas tilted my chin back up so I was looking at him again. "There is not a man here who would stand idly by and let Frank hurt you again. Personally, I would sooner die than let it happen."

I bit the corner of my bottom lip. "Thank you, Phineas."

"Next!" Father shouted. Phineas kissed my forehead gently, then turned to go have his turn.

The men all let me alone for the rest of their turns through the obstacle course. I couldn't see how they all got through it so quickly, even Lucas, who was terrified, made it through pretty quickly.

Of the Princes, Harrison was by far the quickest on the obstacle course, followed, respectively, by Ilya, Alex, Leon, and Phineas.

Of the Arborians, Frank was fastest, followed by Henry, Peter, John, and Lucas.

When everyone had gone through, Peter shouted out, "Rose's turn!" and everyone looked at me expectantly.

I held my arms out, palm up and widened my eyes. "Oh, no. I don't think so."

"Come on, Miriam. Be a sport and have a go!" Phineas shouted. Harrison winked in agreement.

Curse you and your infernal winking.

Harrison laughed at my thought.

I backed away and smirked. "There is no way I am going up that cliff side." I looked at Father for support, but he unhelpfully stood there with his Note-Taker tucked under his crossed arms.

Gee. Thanks, Dad.

Harrison laughed again and I glared at him. I backed into what I thought was a tree, but it turned out to be Lucas. "Come on, Miriam. Your turn." He grabbed my hand and began pulling me over.

"No!" I screamed in mock terror and John took it as his cue to grab my other hand and pull. Next thing I knew, I was potato sacked over Ilya's shoulder and he was setting me down in front of the rock face. When I looked at him, he had a giant smile on his face. He gripped my hips and spun me around so he was behind me.

"It is not so difficult, Miriam. You just look up and keep moving," Ilya whispered into my ear with an amused smile on his lips.

I turned my head to look him in the eye. "Oh. I know how to do it, Ilya. I just do not want to put all you boys to shame."

A chorus of oh's, ah's, and oo's echoed over the men and Father shook his head in amusement. I gave Ilya a quick kiss on the cheek them gently shoved him away. In my false life, I had never done anything like the obstacle course, but every fiber of my being was telling me I did this sort of thing for fun in my real life.

My fingers and toes tingled in anticipation as I rescanned the cliff for the path I had mentally drawn earlier. All the men, except Frank, were chortling and elbowing each other, probably thinking that little ole me was going to need a big strong man to help me get through the course.

Though I had shoved Ilya, he still stood maddeningly nearby. "There is no need to be nervous, Miriam. I will catch you if you fall."

"Oh, will you? I feel *so* much better now." I said as if it really relieved a fear I didn't actually have.

Watch and learn, boys.

I thought this looking straight at Harrison and his eyes widened.

Giving Harrison a mocking wink, I yelled, "Tell me when, Father!" and all the men shouted encouragement.

"Ready. Set. Go!" Father shouted and up I went. Every crevice and dip available found my hands and feet to make a quick climb. Because my feet were pretty small, finding a ledge to get on was easy. My body hummed as I pulled up to the top and the cheers below me grew loud. After blowing the participants a kiss, I rubbed my hands together.

Deciding to show off, I did several round offs over the log and nimbly swung from rope to rope until I lightly landed with a bow. Father announced I had the third highest score, but all the men, besides Frank, insisted I had the highest score because I did it with style.

I shakily looked down at my hands, in absolute wonder at what my body had just done. I thought back to my dance lessons with Doctor Bartholomew. His theory on how even if my mind doesn't remember things, my body must rang true. In my false life, I was probably the least athletic person I knew. Apparently, that wasn't the case in my real life.

Harrison could no longer resist and pulled me into an encircling embrace, which helped me regain my composure. I squealed as he passed me off to John, who passed me on to Ilya and so on, until I ended at Phineas. I noticed he set me down and completely ignored the pouting Frank.

"Excellent job, Miriam," Frank muttered, but didn't dare touch me.

I nodded in gratitude, then walked into a hug from Father, who was very surprised that I had completed the obstacle course. "Clearly, your body remembered doing that sort of thing. I figured it would," Father whispered proudly, confirming my suspicions that this was a normal thing for me to do.

"Back to the tree line, gentlemen. Let us get your lists so we can get the next event going!" Father shouted and gave me his arm as we walked back.

Chapter 13

When we returned to the tree line, Father divvied out Note-Takers that had the list of things to find. The list consisted of basic survival items like firewood, kindling, edible fruits and nuts, blah, blah, blah. A large bonfire would be built to keep them warm for the final part of the day's testing when they all came back from their hunt.

The largest thermos of coffee I had ever seen was waiting for me – I had apparently created a reputation for being a binge coffee drinker in the kitchen – and a nice soft chair had been brought for me to sit in while I waited for the King's Test participants' return.

As I took my seat, Father patted my shoulders and handed me his Note-Taker. "I'm going in for a while." When I turned to face him, I noticed Frank going inside and smiled, thinking he wouldn't get the quickest time if he was going to make a stop at the palace first. Then, what Father said hit me.

"Hold on. You are leaving me out here alone?" I asked.

"You are not alone, Rose. There are nine men that I trust out there and Louis is by the doors to the palace." Father bent over and kissed the top of my head. "I know how introverted you are. I am sure you could use some time to yourself."

I grumbled random nonsense and Father chuckled as he made his way inside. Knowing the men would be some time, I leaned back and closed my eyes, rubbing my arms to try to get warmth. After a few moments, I curled my legs under me to add to it. My boots dug into my rear and I had to put them back on the ground. Getting frustrated with the cold December air, I grunted and heard a familiar laugh behind me.

"This may help keep you warm," Frank said hovering over me. I opened my eyes and he was inches from me.

"While your breath is warm, Frank, it's actually not doing much for me," I muttered.

Frank chuckled and moved in front of me, presenting a replica of the green leather jacket I loved that was ruined when I was shot. Because Frank was the one who had given me the jacket, I was loathe to admit that I missed it. As I considered how to accept the jacket without leading him on, I bit my bottom lip.

"I love when you do that," Frank said.

"What?"

"You bite your lip when you are trying to consider something you think contradicts your feelings."

"I hate that."

"What?"

"That you know me that well."

Frank chuckled again. "It is just a jacket, Miriam. I heard your delirious mutter when you were shot. I know you hate me, but you are cold. Please take it."

I rubbed my arms, really wanting to accept his gift. "If I accept it, it does not mean I am not mad at you for earlier. You were rude."

"I know." He offered no apologies; he was clearly not sorry for his spoken words.

Shooting out a frustrated hand, I accepted the jacket and slipped it on. It felt just as cozy as it did before. After I took the jacket, I saw he had a blanket draped over his arm and he placed it over my legs. "Thanks," I mumbled. Frank kissed the top of my head affectionately, picked up his Note-Taker, and went into the forest.

So frustrated. I should have worn my own coat. Oh well. At least I'm warm now. Harrison, if you can hear me, I would like it if you made it back before Frank. I don't want to be alone with him again any time soon.

As I finished up my giant container of coffee, I closed my eyes. With the amount of caffeine I had just pumped into my system, I have no idea how I managed to go to sleep, but I did.

I stand on a platform between two green silhouettes wearing a nondescript white dress. I know the men are participants of the King's Test. Father and Mother stand in front of us. Though I cannot understand him, I know Father is announcing the winner of the King's Test.

The green silhouette on my right leaves and I turn to the man on my left, ready to take my vows.

The Man of Night appears, enraged, and kills Father and Mother with the same weapon that was used on me during my assassination attempt. I scream.

I woke up screaming and Phineas came bursting through the tree line, soon followed by the other men popping out one by one. After looking around to find nothing really wrong, Phineas walked over and lowered himself to his knees in front of me, cupping my face in his hands.

"Is everything alright, love?" he asked with a furrowed brow.

Trembling, I nodded vigorously. The last thing I needed was someone else being privy to my visions.

"I do not believe you. Would you like me to stay with you?"

"No!" I answered a little too sharply and he quirked a brow at me as he pulled his head back a little. "I mean – No. You need to participate and do well. I – It was only a bad dream. It was nothing." I smiled and noted that he gave me a look indicating he was not convinced.

"Very well. I will be back soon." Phineas gestured to the tree line at his stack of items. "I am almost finished. I promise to be done before Frank, alright?"

"Alright. Thank you," I respond.

With hesitancy, Phineas stood up and went back into the forest. I nibbled at my thumbnail as I considered the vision.

If only I could figure out who the Man of Night is. Then I could stop the vision from coming true. Roots. I couldn't even protect Ella and Thomas and I knew they were the ones in danger. Perhaps it just can't be helped. Maybe the visions are just a way to prepare me for whatever is coming. Maybe –

My thoughts were interrupted by Harrison dropping all of his things in front of me. "Time," he said, breathing heavily with a giant grin on his face. I noted his time on Father's Note-Taker without looking at him or going over his items. Harrison picked up his fire items and moved them away from me a few feet and arranged them in a way to begin the pile for the bonfire.

When he finished, he came back over to me and took my hands. "Do you want to talk about it?"

"What?"

"Your vision. Phineas beat me over here, but I ran back in and finished at breakneck speed so I could return to you."

I placed my palm on his cheek. "What is this, Harrison?" The speed at which our relationship was progressing was terrifying and wonderful all at once. Already, it would be tragic if he didn't end up becoming my King.

Harrison put his hand over mine and pressed his cheek against my palm. "Scary, is what it is. So – tell me."

As I looked into his deep blue eyes, I realized that David hadn't visited my dreams the night before. After Ella and Thomas' deaths, I would have thought he would come to comfort me. I wondered if what I had with Harrison rendered him no longer needed.

"Miriam?"

I blinked a few times to exit my thoughts. "Um – I was standing on stage between two unidentifiable men. Father and Mother stood before us and Father announced who won. The Man of Night was displeased and killed Father and Mother."

"The Man of Night?"

"That was what David called him when I saw him the first time. When he is in my visions, he appears as a black silhouette with stars dispersed within it. Based on a previous vision, he is one of the participants."

"Frank?"

"That was my first thought, but now I'm not so sure. I can't let go of how angry Britainnia was when the foreigners King's Test was cancelled the first time around. Prince George XV even said it could cause international conflict.

"Then Ella and Thomas died and Peter steps in to participate in the King's Test the next day? That is very suspicious to me. It is also suspicious that everyone on the Council was on board with it.

"But, yeah. Frank is still being a scary oddity among you all. But he *did* order his people to respect whoever wins the King's

Test." I rubbed my thumb on Harrison's hand. "I just don't know. It could even be *you* for all I know. I could be doing something monumentally stupid sharing all this with you."

"Hey, now," Harrison said in mock offense. "If there is anyone you can trust, it's me. You asked me what this is? This is me falling in love scary fast with a woman I may not be able to marry. I promise you: I will protect you and look out for you, even if I end up being a total loser in all this." He leaned in and kissed my cheek. "I don't know what I would do if something bad were to happen to you."

Harrison sat down in front of me and kept holding my hand in his. He was so much larger than me, it was almost humorous, but the warmth of his love and body against the cold was better than any fire that would be set that night. "What happened to the winner?"

"What?"

"You said this Man of Night killed your Father and Mother. What happened to the winner?"

I paused and thought back to the vision, realizing a terrifying thought. "I don't know."

Chapter 14

Slowly, the rest of the participants came back and added their fire bundles to the pile. Phineas was true to his word and arrived back before Frank. Frank actually was one of the last men to return and he wasn't very happy about it. By the time Father rejoined us, the fire had been lit and we were all snacking on the berries and nuts the men had brought back with them from their scavenger hunt.

"Alright, men. I am going to escort Crown Princess Miriam to her spot in the woods since it is now dark. I will be back shortly. Please decide your order before I return," Father announced as he took my hands to help me up.

Since I had been sitting for so long, my back popped in at least four different places and the men nearest me chuckled about the loud sound. "Laugh it up, boys. One of you could be the lucky one to get to hear those pops every morning for the rest of your lives." Frank and Peter both snorted at that and I quirked an eyebrow at the strange pair as I went into the forest with Father.

"This may seem like a weird question, Father, but did Peter ever sleep with me?"

Father choked on the air he was breathing. I quickly clarified. "Oh. No. Not *sleep with* me. I mean, sleep with me – like in the same room."

"Rotting roots, Rose! Don't do that to me. You'll give your old man a heart attack." Father placed his hand to his chest. "To answer your question, yes. A couple of times shortly before you went into your freeze. Why do you ask?"

"Oh. He and Frank seemed to share a silent joke when I was talking about my back popping every morning."

"I wouldn't think anything of it," Father said.

"I can't help it. Don't you find this whole thing with Peter suspicious at all?"

"Don't, Rose," Father warned.

"Don't what? Seriously, does Peter seem like a man mourning over his dead wife and son?"

Father stopped and gently held my arms so we were facing each other. "Listen, you don't know what Peter went through all those years you were frozen. He missed you terribly and he obviously never got over you. I trust him completely."

"But is that trust misplaced?"

Father only sighed in response and turned to continue our trek through the forest. We stayed silent the rest of the way into the woods to a spot behind a tree. After the conversation about Peter, I knew Father would not be heeding any warning I gave him. I didn't even bother mentioning Britainnia.

Before leaving, Father handed me a box with little satin roses in it. He instructed me to give one to each man when he found me, then left me alone in the woods. The sky was unusually clear for a December night in Arboria, and the moon was full.

While the jacket had helped with the cold earlier in the day, it had become bitter cold as the evening progressed. Setting the box on the ground, I removed my hair tie and unwove the braid down my left shoulder. Letting it fall down my back and over my shoulders, I shook it out and sighed in relief as the tension of my braid released at the roots. My long tresses began to warm my neck nearly immediately and I was glad I thought to do it.

Not surprisingly, the men sent Frank out first. No doubt the forest was lined with Guards and everyone probably just wanted him out of the way. "I cannot believe your Father left you out here alone after you were kidnapped and there was an explosion a couple days ago."

"Well, *you* are their leader. No one is going to get me while you are still at the palace."

"You think *I* had something to do with the explosion?" Frank asked incredulously.

I took a satin rose out of the box and handed it to him. "Better get back before your time suffers too much."

Snatching the rose from my hand, he said, "This is not over, Miriam. We need to talk about it."

I scoffed as he turned away. "And to think I forgave you. I am ashamed of myself for falling for your lies."

"I have not lied!" he shouted as he got further away.

"Oh! What a lie!" I shouted back and was answered with silence. I knew better than to egg him on. He would certainly find a way to corner me now. As long as I was on Evergreen Palace's grounds, I was safe. I just couldn't let him get me away again.

A while later, Peter showed up and I handed him a rose when he approached. Peter laughed. "Playing up the Rose of Petrichoria thing a little hard, aren't we?"

"It wasn't *my* idea. What? Did the men want you and Frank out of the way? Seems like you two are thick as thieves now."

Peter sighed. "No. I still hate him. We are just both equally detested among the participants." Peter shook his head and left me alone.

I wasn't sure what order they used or how they came up with it, but I was pleased when Phineas was last. Harrison had found me easily enough with my loud thinking, but left with a short peck and without a word.

Though I was loathe to admit it, I was still apprehensive of Phineas because of the memory of his brother. Granted, it wasn't fair for me to judge him based on his brother, but I couldn't help but wonder if his family wasn't behind the mutated Daze that got us to the current King's Test in the first place. Or if they were, if he knew anything about it.

Unfortunately for me, I did find Phineas extremely attractive and he had been kind to me since arriving in Arboria shortly before my birthday. He was one of the only men who came to rescue me out of something besides duty and he had saved me from Frank earlier that day. I didn't know how to feel. If I didn't get to marry Harrison, I felt like Phineas would be a good husband as well – even if I didn't love him.

When Phineas rounded my tree, I handed him my final satin rose and he appropriated the empty box as well. He took my hand and led me along the forest in amiable silence. "Is everything alright with us, Miriam?" he said and broke the quiet night air.

"Of course. Why would they not be?" I responded.

"You have been acting strangely since our interview yesterday. Did I offend you when I did not kiss you?"

I laughed dryly. "No. We are really alright. It has just been a long day. Do you think you fared well in the tests today?"

"I did alright. Not the best, but I will not be going home after today."

"Good. I am glad."

"Unfortunately, Peter and Frank will be staying as well."

I sighed. "Yes. I figured as much. Peter grew up spending time with me in these forests and Frank is – well – more trained in physical survival than most, I think."

After another moment of quiet, Phineas asked, "How do you feel about Peter joining in the King's Test?"

"It disgusts me." I slapped my hand over my mouth, not believing that I was so candid about it. "Please do not tell anyone I said that."

Phineas laughed. "I will not. Though it is strange. Were you two not together before your freeze?"

I nodded. "Yes, but then he married my best friend and had a beautiful family with her. It sickens me that he was so quick to want to remarry after their deaths."

"It sickens us all. He essentially paid off Samuel, too. He told him if he won, he would make sure he was appointed as the new Duke of Maple."

I furrowed my brow. "I didn't figure Samuel to be one for money and title."

"Me neither. To be honest, he probably would have given his spot anyway. Peter and Ella were good to him; he had no reason *not* to be loyal to them."

As we approached the bonfire, the men all erupted in applause and Father noted Phineas' time when he handed over the rose. "I will average out your scores and announce those who will be going home when I figure it out," Father said.

Phineas joined the circle of men around the fire and Frank put the blanket he had brought out for me earlier around my shoulders before standing next to me a few feet away.

"Are you ready to talk about this now?" Frank asked cryptically.

"What?" I responded and snuggled the blanket to my chin – it was very cold.

He stepped a little closer and leaned over to me. "I had nothing to do with that explosion. Why would I possibly want Duchess Elleouise dead? She was your best friend and cousin."

"So I no longer have a confidant? I do not understand the way your twisted mind works, Frank."

He sighed. "You'll never believe me. You'll see. I bet they find out who it was and they aren't connected to me at all."

I sniffed. "I'm sure you covered your tracks well."

Frank threw his arms up in the air with frustration and stomped over to the fire. I thought of my friend and hoped her death was swift – that she didn't feel too much pain and that she was in a place where she didn't have to think about it or what was left behind. I hoped the same thing for her child.

I hardly knew her before she died because of my memory loss and now that I remembered her, I missed everything about her. We would never again lay in a field. She wouldn't be there for advice when I become pregnant someday. She wouldn't be there for me anymore – especially now, during the King's Test, when I really needed her.

Before I knew what was happening, tears filled my eyes and fell down my cheeks. I dried my face with the blanket and when I looked again, Peter was in front of me. "What do you want, Peter?" I asked.

"Do you think I am unaffected, Rose?"

I looked at him in a way to say that was exactly what I thought.

"Well – I'm not. Maybe I never really loved Ella romantically, but she was my best friend, too. And there is a hole left in me by the death of Thomas that can never be filled."

"I can't understand you, Peter. I can't understand how you can still be trying for me."

"I promised you once that I would try my hardest in the King's Test. Now that I'm able, I intend on following through with it, even if you hate me right now for doing it."

I looked at him with my mouth dropped wide open as he took my hand and pulled me into an embrace. Rather than tense up, I relaxed into it. His behavior and declarations were still a bit horrifying to me, but he was right. We both lost a friend in Ella and he lost a son – even if he *was* behind it, he had to be regretting that part.

When Father rejoined us, I separated from Peter and gave him a comforting smile. Though what I really wanted to do was go stand by Harrison, I moved to stand by Father as he made his announcement.

"Gentlemen, I have your scores. The top Prince today was – Prince Harrison." Harrison shook his fists in the air in victory and I smiled at him. "The top Arborian today was – Francis Miller of Elm." Frank simply nodded and shifted uncomfortably on his feet.

"The Prince who will be going home tonight is – Prince Leonardo of Swiss-France." Leon sighed, but nodded. "The Arborian going home tonight is – Lucas Flowers of Willow." Lucas let out the same defeated sigh as Leon and they shook hands.

"The remaining eight men and I will go in for dinner. I will leave the three of you to say your good-byes," Father said and everyone he had ordered to, followed him inside.

First, I went to Leon and he shrugged. "*Ma chérie*, I am sorry I could not perform to the King's Test standards today. Though it seems like your heart is already gravitating towards someone else as it is, *oui*?"

I smiled and nodded. "You performed your best and that was all I could expect. Thank you for finding me worthy of taking a chance." Leon kissed my hand and walked away.

Looking over to Lucas, I saw him smiling sadly at me. "Lucas, I am so happy you faced your fears today. You are going to make some woman a very lucky wife."

Lucas sniffed. "Just not you, huh?"

"Not me, but I hope to be invited to the wedding. And you had better serenade that woman all the way down the aisle."

He laughed. "I will. Thank you for this opportunity, Miriam." Lucas kissed my hand and left me standing alone.

For a while, I just stood there, looking into the fire and considering the men left. I knew who I wanted to win, but wondered at who would be alright, if I couldn't have Harrison.

As if he was reading my thoughts, which he actually probably was, Harrison stepped up behind me, coming back out of the palace. "Miriam?"

"Rose. You can call me Rose. There's no point fighting it, Harrison."

"Rose." Harrison said my name with awe and wonder and took my hand. "You have had a difficult day, but it's not over yet, darlin'."

As he kissed my hand, I said, "I know. Everyone is probably waiting for me in there, huh?"

"Yes'm."

"Did you just call me 'ma'am' in a contraction?"

"Ah – yeah. I guess I did."

I laughed. "As far as I remember, no one has ever used that one with me. Not even in my false life."

"Sorry?"

"No need to be sorry. I needed a good laugh." After a deep sigh, I added, "Alright. Let's go." Hand-in-hand, we walked back into the palace to get some final instructions from Father before getting to bed for the night.

Chapter 15

When we walked into the Core, Lucas and Leon were heading out the front door with their luggage in tow. With a final wave, they strolled out the doors and we were officially down to eight men. Harrison rejoined the line and I joined Father standing in front.

The participants were all clearly exhausted – well – except Alex, who always seemed to have the energy of a five-year-old. Some men were yawning with their mouths closed and others were trying to stretch nonchalantly. We were all ready for bed.

I was regretting my decision to show off earlier. My body was sore in places I didn't know I had and I silently promised myself to begin working out somehow so I wasn't sore the next time. Harrison snorted at my thought, then tried to cover his laugh with a cough when everyone gave him a strange look.

Real smooth, Harrison.

Father began, "Gentlemen, congratulations on passing the first two parts of the King's Test. Things are not going to get easier from here on out. For instance, tonight, we will be starting the next portion of the test."

Peter openly baulked at Father's declaration, while Alex seemed to burst with renewed energy. The other men began rolling shoulders and necks and I could see the day had worn on them as much as it had on me.

"Sometimes as King, you will need to work all day and through the night and still maintain composure, intellect, and proper reflexes. Throughout the night, you will take tests in these categories every so often without warning. If you fall asleep before the tests are complete, you will automatically be disqualified.

"I understand this may seem harsh, but no one will be sympathetic to your sleep deprivation when you become King. What will they care about? Are you responsive in an emergency? Will you make wise decisions even if you have no one available for council? What type of person are you under pressure?

"All these things are important. Tonight's testing will take place in the Royal Library. Follow me."

I walked alongside Father up the Core to the Royal Library, trying not to groan at how tired I was.

I hope I don't have to stay awake, too.

At the thought, I felt the light brush of Harrison's fingers against mine and smiled. Although I was certain it was no mystery to anyone that there was a spark between us, I was glad for him being discreet.

As we walked to the library, Father handed me his Note-Taker. When we entered, I saw a cushy bed against the window and paused. Raising an eyebrow at Father, I asked, "Why is there a bed in here?"

"For you, dear," Father said without further explanation.

The men made their line and Father continued. "Tonight, Crown Princess Miriam will be administering your tests. While you will be staying awake, she will be sleeping nice and cozy in a soft, warm bed." I chortled and Father gave me an amused look.

"Her Guard, Earl, will be responsible for waking her up for your tests and for escorting any of you who fall asleep to your rooms to pack your things. Yes, this means that there could potentially be more than one Prince and more than one Arborian going home after this test."

Kissing the top of my head, Father said, "Good night, Miriam. Good night, gentlemen. I will now be off to spend some well-earned time with my wife."

"Good night, sir," the men said in unison, then split off to grab books and settle in for the night. Before leaving, Father handed me the men's Note-Takers. After doing that, he left without another word.

I shuffled myself over to the bed, wishing I could shower and change into more suitable sleep clothes. Peter laughed when I plopped myself onto the edge of the bed.

"What?" I asked, perturbed.

"Doctor Bartholomew would have your head if he saw you plop like that," he responded.

I smirked. "You are probably right. I can hear him now: 'Princesses don't plop! How many times do I have to tell you?'" I laughed at my terrible impression and Peter laughed, too. Several of the other men smiled, but did not join in our discussion. After all, *they* had no idea who Doctor Bartholomew was.

Peter walked over with a book and placed it on my head. Instantly, my body automatically straightened and a couple of the Princes laughed at my natural reflex. Taking the book from my head, I smiled and stretched saying, "Very funny, Peter."

"How many do you think you can do, Rose?"

I shrugged and yawned my response. "I don't know. I haven't really tried since my recovery. The nurses kept slapping Doctor Bartholomew's hands away."

Harrison walked over with four books. "Let's find out."

I raised a brow at him and leaned forward, elbows on my knees. "Are you serious? I am supposed to be sleeping. I am not here for everyone's entertainment."

"Aw. Come on, Miriam. Let us see!" Alex said from the other side of the room. Ilya and Frank remained silent and seated, but smiled behind books.

"Fine, but not all those at once," I mumbled, straightening my posture. Henry and John shouted hoorays and Phineas made his way over with more books. "After this, though, I *will* be going to sleep. I like you all, but it is not *my* responsibility to stay awake all night and perform tricks for your amusement."

As Peter placed the first book on my head, Phineas, Harrison, Alex, Henry, and John made a semi-circle in front of me. They each took turns placing books on my head. The most I had done before that night was five. When John placed the sixth on my head, I held my breath. After a few moments, I slowly released my breath and the men cheered like it was a bar game and they were all going to get a shot of whiskey.

"Let us make this interesting," Ilya said. I had been so busy maintaining my posture, I hadn't heard or seen him come over.

Looking up with my eyes, I asked, "What do you mean?"

Ilya squatted so he could look me in the eyes. "Six books is impressive, Miriam. I am sure with your grace, we could probably stack books on your head all night and your posture would be as straight."

A couple of the guys groaned at the compliment and I pressed my lips together to suppress a giggle that might make the books fall.

"I am afraid, though, your neck might not be able to handle too many more books. You are still recovering, yes?"

"Uh-huh. But I am basically back to normal."

"Excellent." Ilya stood and offered me his hand. "I will help you stand."

"You are wanting me to walk with these on my head?" I asked as I carefully stood without his assistance.

Gently tugging me over to himself, he positioned us for a waltz. I widened my eyes. "No way. I have never danced with books on my head," I said as I realized what he was doing. Then, I realized I remembered that I really hadn't ever done that.

"YES!" shouted Alex like a child who won the candy jackpot. He practically skipped his way over to a desk and put on some song in 3/3 that I had never heard. "We will each take a turn."

"Ugh. Fine. One dance each, then I *am* going to sleep. For reals."

"For reals?" Phineas asked, scrunching up his nose.

"Oh stop. I am sure you have slang in Britainnia."

Frank chuckled. Removing my hand from Ilya, I wagged a finger at Frank. "Oh. You just wait. You will get yours."

"I look forward to it," Frank laughed and everyone laughed with him. We were at the I-am-so-tired-everything-is-funny stage of the night.

Placing my hand back on Ilya's shoulder, I said, "Alex, restart the song. Let us do this."

I made it through the first waltz relatively easily. Each man danced with me, even Frank, and we all had more fun than we had originally anticipated for the night. With a flourished curtsey, I removed the books from my head and all the men cheered and applauded.

I rolled my neck. "Alright, boys. I am going to bed now." I made a pointed look at Phineas. "For reals!"

Phineas laughed and offered his arm to escort me to the bed. Harrison pulled the blankets back while John punched the pillows. When I sat, Henry got down on his hands and knees and removed my boots. "Guys. This really is not –"

"Nonsense, Rose," Peter interrupted me with a solemn expression. "You have no Crown Princess' Maiden tonight to help you." I met his watery gaze at the reminder of who was missing from the King's Test proceedings. Quickly recovering, he added, "You have been forced to spend the evening with eight annoying men. Besides, I don't think you can remove your own shoes." Henry chuckled and I yanked my feet up onto the bed.

Laying on my side and facing the window, I yawned and said, "Good night, participants."

Someone lowered the lights and I felt someone kiss the top of my head. Then another. Then six more. By the time the final chaste kiss came, I was asleep.

Chapter 16

I let out a deep sigh as I snuggle into David on a sofa in the empty Royal Library.

"I thought you were done with me," I say to him as I nuzzle into his side.

"I thought you were done with me," David responds. "Remember how this works? I'm a figment of your imagination. I come when you need me."

"That's right," I mumble. "I'm sorry."

"Why?"

"I think I forgot about you for a while."

David laughs. "It wouldn't be so bad. That Harrison guy seems nice."

I frown. "It feels weird to talk about other men with you." I sigh. "I miss Ella."

David kisses the top of my head. "I know."

"Do you think she's in a better place?"

"Yes."

"Good. Because if you think it, I probably know it subconsciously."

David chuckles. "You think too much, Miriam. But I'm pretty sure something is going on. You should wake up."

"Miriam?" Henry was gently shaking me and kneeling beside me. When I looked at him, he looked sad and Earl was standing behind him.

"What's going on, Henry?" I asked groggily.

"I – fell asleep. Earl left me alone for a while to wake up on my own, but after thirty minutes, he had to tell me I need to leave."

"Oh, Henry. I'm so sorry," I said, placing a hand on his cheek.

"Honestly, I'm dependable. I – I don't know what happened."

"I'm sure you are."

Henry kissed my hand and said goodbye. Earl walked him out and all the men were pretty somber.

"What time is it?" I asked no one in particular.

"3:00 in the morning," Frank answered.

"No tests yet?"

"No ma'am," Harrison said with a tired smirk.

"Huh."

I turned back over and looked out the window. The dim green light from the Space Needle shone comfortingly and made me feel safe.

Though I had been glad to visit with David, it made me sad to realize I still needed him.

Perhaps when I marry, I will no longer need him.

After I had the thought, I knew it would be bugging Harrison to know who I was thinking of, but it didn't bother me. What did bother me was the realization that nothing was private for me anymore. I trusted Harrison, but it would have been nice at least be able to be alone at least in my head.

Just before I fell asleep again, the holocomm lit up with Father's face and Earl re-entered the room. "Rose? Rose?" Father sounded frantic, so I leaped out of bed and rushed over to the library's holostation.

"What's going on, Father?"

"There are intruders. We don't know who –"

The power shut off and, thus, ended our conversation. There was no light in the room besides the green light of the Space Needle. Whatever was going on, it wasn't known to the public and we had no way of getting any more information.

"Earl, use the manual locks on the doors, please," Frank said, clearly familiar with the palace's security measures from his time as a Guard. Without question, Earl locked the doors. I looked around the room. Alex no longer seemed happy, he seemed panicked, as did John. Ilya looked like he was about to explode with anger.

"We need to get out of here," Peter said.

"Does the palace have safe rooms?" Harrison said. Frank and Peter both nodded.

"Miriam, step away from the windows. Come over here with us," Phineas said. I walked over to the corner where the men were all standing.

Ilya snapped his fingers several times. "Where are the safe rooms, Frank?"

"There are several. I know there is one down at the end of this branch."

"That would require us leaving the room. Is there not anything in the room? We have intruders out there!" Ilya was shouting and Harrison shushed him.

"I'm confused. It's so quiet. Why isn't there more noise if there are intruders?" I asked.

As if on cue, the sound of screaming and shouting shot up from the Core. We heard the sound of heavy footsteps approaching then banging on the door.

"Open up! We know the Crown Princess is in there and we are here to take her."

My eyes widened and I shot a terrified look at Frank. He raised his hands. "It's not me. It's possible it's my people, but I had nothing to do with it."

Ilya grabbed Frank by the collar and shoved him against the wall. "Why should we believe you, traitor?"

"You have no reason to, but I have no reason to lie, either. If I knew what was going on, wouldn't I be joining in with the intruders? I would have the upper hand here."

Ilya pursed his lips and glared at him. "Frank is right. It would not make sense. As much as I loathe the creature, I do not think he is behind what is going on here," Phineas tried to reason with Ilya, but Ilya wasn't having any of it and only tightened his grip.

The banging on the door got louder. "We need to get Miriam to safety. Peter, Frank, do you know if there is an escape from here?" Harrison asked.

Still being held up by Ilya, Frank shrugged and I hated that I was so useless because of my memory problems. Harrison put a protective arm around my waist as Peter spoke suddenly, as if just remembering something. "I know of one. I used to use it to sneak in here when we were teenagers."

Peter rushed over to a wall and skimmed the books until finding a rather large volume and pulled on it. The bookshelf slid open to become a doorway. I began to make my way over to it, but was shoved out of the way by John, who raced out in terror, Alex close behind him. Harrison was right behind me and caught me before I hit the floor.

"Cowards!" Ilya shouted behind them as he abruptly released Frank to shake his fist in their direction. Frank's feet hit the floor hard with a thud and he grunted.

"I can't believe they pushed you out of the way like that!" Peter said in anger, rushing over to me and giving me a quick once-over.

"Forget it. Let's get Miriam out of here!" Harrison shouted over the ever-increasing volume of banging on the door. When we got halfway down the stairs in the tunnel, we heard Alex and John shout in surprise and we all froze.

Harrison gently pushed me against the wall and the men made a cocoon of safety around me by blocking me in. I could no longer see what was going on, but felt the tension ease in Harrison's back when my Father said, "Well done, most of you."

"Father?" I said from behind my human wall. Harrison moved so I could walk forward. "What's going on here?"

"The test. Prince Alexander and John have failed and will be going home."

"I am sorry. I am ashamed of the cowardice I just displayed," said Alex.

"Me too. I do not know what came over me," added John.

The two of them were ashamed of themselves, as they should have been. It was a good test, I thought. Had they been notified about a false attack, the reactions would not have been genuine. Earl escorted the men from the stairway, leaving only five participants left.

Turning to face Frank, Ilya said, "Francis, please accept my apologies. I should not have jumped to conclusions."

"Forget about it. I probably would have thought the same thing," Frank replied with a frown. The two men shook hands.

I couldn't believe how fast everything had happened and I suddenly felt feint and overwhelmed. Harrison noticed and placed a sturdy hand around my waist. Father noticed, as well.

Father said, "Rose, I will let you choose an escort to walk with you to your room. Everyone else can go get some rest. Tonight, there will be a party in the ballroom. All the Nobility and Delegates will be in attendance, so you will want to be at your best tomorrow. It will begin at 7:00 in the evening. Dinner will be brought to your rooms."

The five participants left looked at me expectantly, though it should have been obvious who my choice would be. "I choose Harrison to walk back with me."

"So shocked," Peter muttered. Ilya elbowed him hard and grinned at me when Peter grunted.

"I would also like it if I could see all five participants tomorrow before the party. Get to know you each a little better."

"Even Frank?" Peter asked and got elbowed again by Ilya. That time, Peter shot him a glare.

"Yes. Even Frank. Frank, you will meet with me from 10:00-11:00. Harrison from 11:30-12:30. Peter from 1:00-2:00. Ilya from 2:30-3:30. And Phineas from 4:00-5:00. That leaves plenty of time for getting ready for the party."

"Where will we meet?" Phineas asked.

"Up in my room will be fine. Good night, gentlemen. I will see you later." Harrison kept his arm around me in support as we made our way back up the stairs, through the library, and up the Core to my room. I was feeling weak from the adrenaline rush and the long day.

"So – who were you thinking about earlier?" Harrison asked as if he was wondering what the color of the clouds would be later on in the day. Because I knew it had been driving him crazy, I smirked. "Rose?"

"My late husband visited me in a dream."

Harrison furrowed his brow. "In your dream? Does that happen often?"

"Not so much anymore. I can only assume he made an appearance tonight because I realized he didn't visit me when Ella died last night. It is unusual for him to not come to me when I need someone to talk with."

"Hmm. Did you ask him about it?"

I stopped our walk at the top of the Core and looked into his eyes. "I love that about you."

Harrison gave me a crooked smile. "What?"

"That you just accept me and all my craziness. That you know about my false life and talk with me as if it was a real one."

He traced his finger along my jaw. "Well, it *was* real – for you." I smiled and we resumed walking.

"To answer your question, he said he didn't come because he thought I was finished with him."

"Why did he think that?"

"Because of you."

"He knows about me? How does he feel about it? I would be pretty jealous."

I laughed and allowed Harrison to escort me into my room. After the door closed behind us, I leaned against the door and took both his hands in mine. "Of course he knows about you. He resides in my mind, so he knows everything I do. As for how he feels about it, David says he wants me to fall in love. He wants me to be so happy that I don't need him anymore."

"I'm so glad I'm not you."

"Me, too." I smiled at him and he gave me one in return.

Pulling me against him, he cupped my face in one of his hands and I leaned my cheek into it. "You have to deal with so much alone."

"Not for long. Within a few days I'll be engaged." I sighed. "They'll probably push the wedding up, too, if my father has his way."

"Hopefully I will be the one at the altar with you. I can't believe how quickly I've fallen for you, Rose." In the next breath, he captured my lips with his. It was incredible to me how familiar Harrison's lips felt against mine, prodding me to move in his rhythm. I loved the feeling of being in his big arms. My heart felt so full in that moment that I could barely breathe.

When he ended our kiss, he pressed his forehead to mine. "I should probably go," Harrison said.

"Yeah. We'll eat lunch while you're here."

"Alright." Harrison gave me another peck, spun me around and walked out the door.

Happily humming to myself, I took a quick shower and put on some night clothes. By the time I climbed into bed, the dim green light of the Space Needle had been replaced by a bright pink dawn. I smiled to myself as I realized that if I ended up with Harrison, the King's Test would have worked out well for me after all.

Chapter 17

"Good morning, Miriam," Adele sang as she walked into my room, chipper as ever.

After a long groan, I said, "Adele, we need to talk about your ungodly cheerfulness in the morning."

Adele only laughed at me. "It is 9:00 in the morning, Miriam!"

"What!?" I shot out of bed and raced over to my closet where she was casually skimming through my clothes. "I have a meeting at 10:00! Didn't anyone tell you?"

Adele scoffed and looked at me in disbelief. "You do not think I can get you ready in an hour?"

"Not at all. I doubt that I will have time left after you are finished to prepare myself mentally for an hour and a half with *Francis*."

"I cannot believe he has made it this far."

"I can't believe he's made it this far without the need for rigging it," I responded.

"Well, he would not have made it past the first round if it were not for the rigging," Adele pointed out.

I sighed. "You are right, of course. Let us get me dressed so I can get my meeting with Frank over with."

"I am sure he is considering it a date with his future wife," Adele teased, waggling her eyebrows at me.

Faking a gag, I said, "Do not even joke about such things."

Laughing, she handed me a forest green halter dress with an ivory cardigan. "Can we do something red today? I need some change. Would it be so bad to have something blue or pink or yellow in my wardrobe?"

"It is –"

" – tradition. I know. Please? Red?"

Adele sighed and took back the green dress, exchanging it for a similar wine red dress. Dangling the dress from one hand, she quipped, "Happy?"

"Yes," I said with a smile the size of the moon.

Rolling her eyes, she assisted me out of my simple nightgown and into a corset, slip, and my dress. After around an hour, she finished with my hair and makeup and helped me into a cardigan with matching ivory heels. "I hate heels," I lamented, remembering the horrible night of my kidnapping when they caused me so much grief.

"I understand, but Doctor Quincy said you are well enough to not have to walk around in flats anymore. The heels are so pretty on you with those long legs."

I gasped as I got hit with a memory.

I am in Peter's arms and he's young, like me. He is smiling at me mischievously.

"How could I resist looking at your long legs and lithe arms?"

"I'm 5'4", Peter. How long can my legs really be?"

He shrugs. "They're lovely all the same."

I roll my eyes, but can't help blushing as I point at him. "Alright, Peter. I can't fault you for that. But no more. You be a gentleman."

He nods and jokes in a snooty voice. "Yes, of course. I must prepare myself for the King's Test."

Though I had been smiling with him, my smile quickly fades and I look down. "Why did you have to go and bring that up?"

He tilts my chin so I am looking at him. A tear falls from my eye before I can stop it and he wipes it away with his thumb. "I'm sorry, Rose. I didn't mean to spoil our meeting. Please forgive me. I'm sorry."

I sniffle most romantically and we both laugh. Blinking away my tears, I tell him it is alright and kiss him.

I woke up still standing with a pained expression.

"Miriam? Are you alright?" Adele asked, concern spread all over her face.

"I – I think so, yes."

I should tell her about my memories. No. I can't tell anyone. The only reason Harrison knows is because he would know regardless. Roots! He's probably so worried right now.

The door chimed and Adele opened it to admit Frank into the room. Before he made it two steps, Adele put her hand up to stop him. "Listen here, Frank. You two may be alone right now, but Louis is right outside. If she so much as makes a peep about you being unkind or rude in any way, he will escort you out of here. Do you understand?"

Frank's eyes widened. "Et tu, Adele?"

"Ironic coming from you, do you not think?" Adele retorted.

I cleared my throat and the pair looked at me. "It is alright, Adele. Frank will behave."

Adele held up two fingers, pointed to her eyes with both, then pointed to him with one as she left. I was still feeling shaky from my memory, so I took a seat on my sofa and gestured for Frank to join me. I curled my legs beneath me and leaned against the arm of the sofa. Frank sat next to me and coolly put an arm around me, as if it was the most natural thing in the world for him to do.

Looking at me, he said, "I'm surprised you included me in today."

Avoiding eye contact, I found a loose string in the sofa and picked at it. As the memory of our time in a similar situation hit me, my heart started racing. With a shrug that belied how I really felt, I answered, "There really was not a way not to."

"I wish you wouldn't do that?"

"Do what?

"Speak to me so formally. It feels weird."

"You having your arm around me feels weird."

Frank gave me a shrug, as well, and nudged a little closer, "You could have left me out," he said, ignoring my comment completely. "Phineas, Harrison, Ilya, and Peter all know who I am and what I did. And I'm sure your father would have understood. I think you're giving me more than is required. Why would that be, Rose?"

"Miriam," I corrected and looked at him.

"Miriam," he repeated with a grin.

Carp. He knew that would get my attention.

"Do you seriously think that, Frank? That I am giving you more than I have to? Because that would be certifiably insane."

Frank nodded. "I don't get it myself. It makes no sense to me."

"Let me let you in on a little something, Frank. Any rigging that there has been for you, is now over because you are in the final two Arborians."

Frank chuckled. "Well, let's be real, Ro – I mean, Miriam. I really only needed it for the first round."

"You are a bit cocky, are you not?"

"I have no reason not to be."

I squinted at him. "What do you have up your sleeve?"

"Absolutely nothing." Finally, he broke his unwavering gaze and looked around. Finding Adele's *Lord of the Rings*, he asked, "What's this?"

"A classic," I responded, glad for the change in subject.

For the rest of his time, we talked about literature of the twentieth and twenty-first centuries. He made recommendations of modern books based on what I told him I liked back in my false life. At 11:00, Louis opened the door.

"Time's up, Frank," Louis said, glaring at Frank. Any doubt I had lingering concerning Louis' loyalty melted away at the death look he dealt Frank in that moment. Frank must have noticed it, too, because I heard him gulp loudly. I also noted that he didn't correct Louis to call him "Francis."

"See you tonight, Frank."

"Tonight, Miriam," Frank kissed my hand and left.

As soon as Frank was gone, I rushed over to the holostation and made orders for Harrison and my lunches. I cleared the small coffee table and waited for the food to arrive. The kitchen staff arrived a few minutes before noon and rushed to get us set up. Harrison arrived just as the last member of the kitchen staff was leaving.

Looking at the special food I had ordered, Harrison said, "What's all this?"

"I told you we would have lunch together," I responded as I walked up to him and gave him a short kiss – I silently thanked Adele for the heels. It was easier to kiss him that way.

"Thank Adele for me, too," Harrison said. I blushed and pulled away, taking his hand and walking him to the table. "Seriously, though. You didn't have to go through all this."

"I thought you might be missing home, so I figured I would have the staff cook up some Southland cuisine. Granted, *they* are probably just as familiar with it as I am, so it won't be exactly like home, but –"

Harrison interrupted me with a kiss and smirked. "Can you get any more perfect?"

I took a seat and Harrison sat, too. As he began to eat, I said, "I'm not perfect. Far from it."

Swallowing his bite, he said, "You have yet to be anything but perfect as far as I'm concerned."

I snorted as I picked up the tortilla-wrapped food that smelled like a burrito, though it had a different name, and took a bite. "Hmm. It *is* a burrito," I muttered with the bite still in my mouth.

"Ah. A crack in your perfection," Harrison teased. "These *used* to be called burritos a long time ago. I can't remember why we stopped calling them that."

"A rose by any other name would smell as sweet."

"Of course you would make a rose comparison."

I raised my brows in surprise. "Don't tell me you've never read or watched *Romeo and Juliet* by Shakespeare."

"The name sounds familiar, but –"

I removed his burrito from his hand and put it back on his plate. Taking his hand, I forced him to stand. "What are you doing?" Harrison asked.

"*We* are going to the library to find a movie of *Romeo and Juliet*."

"Do we even have time? I'm still hungry," Harrison complained.

I opened the door. "Louis, can you find someone to bring our food down to the library?" Louis nodded and I ran down the Core, yanking Harrison behind me. When we reached it, I pressed the button to black out the windows and called up one of many variations of *Romeo and Juliet* with the Desk Computer.

After pushing Harrison onto the couch, I sat down next to him and cuddled into him the way I had with David in my dream – it felt just as right. "Play movie," I said and the movie began.

As we watched the movie, Harrison stroked my long hair and I mouthed certain lines in the movie. Before it was over, I heard, "Poor Harrison! You're making him sit through *Romeo and Juliet*?" It was Peter. Without asking, he plopped down next to me on my other side. "Stop movie," Peter added. "I am not going to sit through this movie again, Rose."

"It's not bad. I kind of liked it," Harrison defended.

"He had never heard of it, so I figured I needed to show him," I said.

"Well, I have seen it one too many times," Peter laughed. "You used to make me watch this with you when we were together." Noticing how close Harrison and I were, Peter threw Harrison's arm off me. "Time's up, cowboy. Catch ya later," Peter said with a mock southern accent.

"Alright, Alright," Harrison said. Before he could stand up, I kissed him softly and it made him smile.

"Out," Peter said, annoyed.

With a smug grin, Harrison strode out the door. I watched the door until it slid all the way closed, then turned my attention over to Peter – he was giving me a dirty look. "What?" I asked.

"You, of anyone, should know better, Rose," Peter said, exasperated.

"I don't know what you mean."

Peter took my hand. "Listen, I know I'm not your favorite person right now, but I also know you don't remember anything from before. Falling in love before the King's Test is complete could end up with you heartbroken. I can't see you go through that."

"It's too late for that."

"I know. I can tell. Harrison is a good man and I don't fault you at all for falling for him, but just prepare yourself for if he doesn't win."

"That's not bad advice," I hated to admit it. "Peter, I have something to tell you. Don't tell anyone, please."

"Of course. You can trust me with anything."

"I have had more memories trickling in."

"What? When? What else have you remembered?"

"When Ella died, I remembered my whole history with her. Today, I had a memory of you here in the library."

Excited and interested, Peter turned to me and leaned his elbows on his legs. "What was the memory?"

"We were getting ready to leave here and I was chastising you about something that had to do with you admiring my body. We teased a bit, then it got serious when you made a joke about the King's Test. I started crying, you apologized, I kissed you, then we left."

Peter nodded sadly. "I remember that. I had shown up unexpectedly and caught you when you fell from a ladder. It was a hot night, so your nightgown was *very* tiny and you were freaking out about it."

"Oh. That's embarrassing," I said, feeling the blood rush to my face.

Peter tentatively cupped my face in his hands. "That's the kind of thing I've been trying to tell you, Rose. You and I had something special before. I know if I win, we'll eventually have something special again."

My voice shaking, I said, "By this request, I am *not* saying I am falling for you again." I took a deep breath. "But can you tell me some things about our history? Maybe it will jog my memory."

Smiling, Peter bent closer and kissed my forehead. "I would love to," he said.

The rest of our time was spent by Peter telling me stories that were familiar to me, but they still felt like they belonged to someone else. He reminisced about us alone and with our friends. He told me about Stephan and who he was to me. Stephan was apparently like a brother to me. Tragically, we shared that we loved each other the day he died. Peter didn't give up on me even then.

When his time was up, I had a better picture of who Peter and I were together. I still thought it was distasteful, his joining in on the King's Test so shortly after Ella and Thomas' deaths, but understood why he did it. He walked me back to my room and kissed me on the cheek before he left.

I had a half hour before Ilya was due to arrive, so I decided to do part of Adele's job for her. I walked into my closet and looked through my wardrobe. It didn't matter how long I was there, I didn't think I would ever get used to having so many pretty things. I spent the whole half hour in there, but was unable to make any decision – it gave me a little more respect for Adele.

When the door chimed, I let Ilya in. He was all business again and I missed the fun Ilya from the night before; the one who had insisted I dance with books on my head. As the door closed, he walked past me towards the sofa in a masculine strut. Observing him sit down and cross a leg, I tilted my head like a curious cat.

"What is it, Miriam?" Ilya asked.

"I am not all that sure what to expect from you, Ilya."

"How do you mean?"

I walked over and sat on the opposite side of the small sofa. I brought my legs up beneath me and faced him. "Well, on the occasions where we have spoken, you have been stoic twice and playful twice. Now, you come here and it is all back to business. Tell me, which is the real Ilya?"

"Both."

"Both?"

"Whether or not I keep my emotions in check varies depending on the circumstance."

"Hmm. So why are you keeping them in check now? Do you not feel like you can be yourself with me?"

He chuckled and a small smile spread across his face as he looked at his hands. "To be honest, I am afraid *not* to keep my emotions in check when I am alone with you."

"Afraid? You?"

Ilya switched his gaze to me. "When I was first invited to come here by your father, I was not afraid. I was excited to leave Northern Europia to meet you. Arranged marriages are common enough in my kingdom, so the concept of marrying a woman I did not love was not something I was opposed to.

"But then I actually met you that night of the interview. Do you remember our first kiss?"

"It was only a couple of nights ago, Ilya," I said with a smile.

"So it was. I did learn something about you; and lost my heart to you in the process."

My eyes widened. "Oh." After swallowing, I asked, "What did you learn?"

"That beyond being beautiful, you have intelligence and opinion, but you are not closed off to people. You were diametrically opposed to the first kisses, but you did it to respect your father and his tradition. It was not all objective, though. There is something wonderful about your spirit. You seem like a good compliment for me."

"Thank you, Ilya." I didn't really know what else to say to that.

He chuckled again. "I know you are not in love with me. I am not asking you to be. I just wanted to be honest with you. Have you studied much about Northern Europia?"

Grateful for the subject change, I told him I hadn't and he told me about his home. It was unsurprising to me how easily that part of the country had switched back over to a monarchical form of government. Unlike Arboria, they didn't have elected officials to run the government with the King.

When his time was up, he kissed my cheek and said he would see me later. I stared at the door and the reality of everything hit me. I didn't feel like Royalty; I still felt like a widowed stay at home mother of one. Oh, I had gotten good at *acting* like I knew what I was doing, like I should be there, but I didn't feel like it.

What would happen when I became Queen if I still didn't have my memories back? I only hoped it would never come to that.

Not much later, Phineas came in the door and had an unusual smile on his face. Taking my hand, he walked me further into the room, but didn't lead me to a seat. "What is that look on your face?" I asked.

"Just excited to finally be alone with you in a situation outside of the King's Test." Phineas' smile widened.

"That's not all. I can tell."

"Alright. I am also happy that I am so close to possibly becoming your husband."

"Ah. I kind of figured it was something like that." I took a seat on the sofa and pulled him to sit next to me. The smile couldn't be wiped from his face.

"Miriam, I know you feel like you are in love with Harrison," Phineas began. I started to say something, but he pressed a finger to my lips. "I understand. It was bound to happen to one of us participants, but I feel like you should know that *I* have fallen for *you*."

"Oh." Once again, I found myself speechless. How was it possible for so many men to fall in love with me in so short a time? One or more of them *had* to be lying about it, but I wasn't sure what they thought they would benefit from it. It's not like I had any say in who would be declared the winner.

Phineas chuckled. "I am not trying to make you feel uncomfortable, Miriam. I am just letting you know that if you end up with me as your husband, you will be getting a man who loves you. I know that was something you feared."

I swallowed hard. "I suppose that means you would like to kiss me now," I said nervously.

"I would love nothing more, Miriam, but I will not do it."

"Why?"

"Because you are not mine yet. But, if I become your fiancé, I *will* kiss you then."

"If? You don't think you will win?"

"First, I hate to think of it as winning. You are not a prize. Second, I am not so full of myself to think I stand any more of a chance than anyone else. Although, I am certain I have more of a chance than Frank."

I laughed dryly. "I certainly hope so – Frank – he scares me."

Phineas entwined his long, lean fingers with my small ones. "I know."

"He *cannot* win. He would be terrible for my kingdom. I do not even want to imagine what he would do to it."

"Or you," Phineas added as he brushed a lock of hair behind my ear. He sighed. "I know you wanted me here for a lot longer, but I need to make a few comms before the party this evening. Would it be alright if I left a little early?"

I shrugged, but the action contradicted the shock of his sudden departure. "I suppose."

Phineas kissed my hand and took his leave. Because he left early, I took advantage of the moments to myself to relax and close my eyes for a bit.

Chapter 18

Peter and I are sitting underneath a willow tree by the banks of a river in the forest behind Evergreen Palace. No. We're not just sitting. I am sitting in his lap and we're kissing.

As Peter moves from my lips to my neck, I say breathlessly, "We really should not be doing this, Peter. My parents will kill *me."*

Peter pulls back and looks me in my eyes with his chocolate brown ones. "They do not have to know."

"We have only just met last night."

"We have known each other a lot longer than that." Peter traces patterns on my back as he continues to hold me close.

"Only by name." Peter smiles the way he did at the ball the previous night – the smile that stole my heart. "What have you done to me Count Peter of Juniper? What magic have you used on me to make me fall for you so fast?"

"Why, Princess, I have done nothing but use my chivalry and charm on you."

Smiling, he pulls me in to continue the kiss.

"Miriam? Rise and shine, dear. Time to get ready for the party."
Adele woke me up from my nap. Looking over to the bed, I saw the
dress she had chosen. I stretched and stood.

"We do not have a lot of time. I sent away dinner, figuring you
would want to skip it in favor of more sleep," Adele said.

"You were right to do it. Let us quickly get ready."

Adele helped me into the new dress. It was an ivory long sleeve
number, tight on top and belled out at the hip. The hem just barely
grazed the floor with the red heels Adele selected. She touched up
my makeup and ran a brush through my hair, then gently placed my
tiara on my head. After pulling on the ivory elbow-length gloves she
handed me, I admired her handiwork in the mirror. "Stunning as
always, Adele. Thank you."

In a rare moment of formality, Adele dipped in a curtsey and
waited for me to leave. When I walked out of my room, I was
surprised to see all five participants of the King's Test waiting for
me. They all wore matching brown pinstripe suits with green vests
and ivory ties.

"What are you all doing here?" I asked, eyeing Earl, who smiled
at me.

"We all wanted to escort you tonight, alone. But rather than
fight each other, we decided that we would all escort you," Peter
said.

"Oh. But on whose arm will I be?" I asked. It was nice that they
were mature enough not to fight, but I didn't have five arms.

"Mine," Harrison said as he stepped forward and offered me his
arm. As I accepted his arm, Phineas flanked him, Peter stood on my
other side, Ilya stood on Peter's other side, and Frank stood behind
us. It seemed as though they all knew who would have won had it

been my choice. Ilya, Peter, and Phineas seemed alright with the knowledge, but Frank's frustration was only thinly veiled.

We had to break formation to descend the Core, but entered into the Main Ballroom back in it. At our entrance, the herald announced us as "Crown Princess Miriam Petrichoria of Arboria and the final five participants of the King's Test: Prince Harrison of Southland, Prince Phineas of Britainnia, Prince Ilya of Northern Europia, Duke Peter of Maple, and Francis Miller of Elm." All the Nobles and Delegates in attendance applauded and Father waited for us at the bottom of the stairs.

As we approached him, Harrison, Phineas, Ilya, and Peter fell back into a line with Frank behind me. Everyone went back to their discussions and the music resumed quietly as background noise. "Tonight, Crown Princess Miriam will introduce you to the Delegates and Nobles of Arboria. Be yourselves and try to have fun." Father gave his brief instructions, took Mother's hand and began his own rotation around the room.

Turning around to face my gentlemen, I sighed and said, "Well, this should be fun." Peter snorted, knowing better. The Delegates and Nobles were a stuffy bunch. Something in my memory just beyond my reach told me that it hadn't always been that way, but there was nothing to be done about it at the moment. I would have to try to reform relations between everyone when I became the one in charge. For the moment, I would just have to endure things the way they were.

We walked around the room making introductions and having polite conversation. All the men laid on the charm thickly, but it was obvious by the body language of everyone that Phineas was a favorite. I wasn't surprised. His accent was something I could sit and listen to all day and he was very good at being formal.

The biggest surprise to me was the cold shoulder everyone seemed to be giving to Peter. Considering how only a few days before, he had a unanimous vote to participate, the fact that no one wanted anything to do with him was a bit of a shock. What was also confusing was that everyone, particularly the Nobles, seemed absolutely delighted with Frank, the traitor.

Despite the fact that Harrison was my favorite and I did my best to talk him up, the Delegates and Nobles seemed to look down their noses at him. Perhaps his accent threw them off. Or his relaxed demeanor. I wasn't sure what it was, but they all seemed to be passive aggressive with him in a quite rude way, implying he was ignorant or stupid.

The Delegates and Nobles were polite with Ilya, but for some reason, he didn't seem to make a lasting impression. Actually, the Delegates seemed to like him well enough, but the Nobles all seemed indifferent.

Once the introductions were complete, the six of us split up. I walked over to my parents and we observed the men as they made their way over to people on their own. When I got to Mother, she hugged me tightly, expressing how much she had missed me over the last few days. "Oh, Rose! I must introduce you to Braedon Tailor. His name is quite appropriate considering his job."

Mother hauled me away from Father, who looked at me sympathetically. When Mother got me over to the gentleman in question, he bowed low. "Your Crowned Highness, it is a pleasure to finally meet you in person. The Queen has told me so much about you."

My eyes widened at the tall, slim man with blond hair tied back at the nape of his neck. I looked over to Mother for help. "This is Braedon Tailor of Petrichoria. He is making your wedding dress for Saturday."

I coughed at what she had just said. "Excuse me?"

Father must have figured out what was going on because he started to make his way across the room to us. Mother began babbling, "Well, I know you like Adele, but she has been working closely with him today and had passed on your likes and dislikes as far as fashion is concerned and –"

"That is not what I am confused about," I said as Father got to me. "Please excuse me Mr. Tailor. I believe I have an important meeting with the King now. I look forward to working with you."

I gripped Father's offered arm as he escorted me from the ballroom down to his office. When his door slid closed, I crossed my arms over my chest. "Saturday? I am getting married on Saturday?! When were you going to tell me this?" I demanded.

Father cleared his throat. "When the winner is announced tomorrow evening."

"Tomorrow – I thought the winner was going to be *announced* on Saturday!"

"Yes, that was before we were able to eliminate one man early and to throw this party two nights early."

I froze and firmly placed my hands on my hips. With a steely voice, I asked, "What do you mean 'this party?'"

Father looked at me with a face full of guilt. I exploded. "This is a test?! What is the test here, Father?"

"It was the compromise for allowing me to eliminate ten up front, Rose. I had to agree to let them decide on the eliminations this round."

"*They* are choosing? No! You can't let them!"

"I have no choice in the matter, dear. It was decided days ago."

"And you didn't think to tell me? Didn't you think I had some right to know?"

"No. This is the *King's* Test, Rose. You have had far too much say in the matter as it is."

"Far too much – Are you serious? This is *my* life we are talking about. Those wretched politicians and Nobles don't care about me at all and they can't stand Harrison. They are going to send him home, Father!" I was crying now. "I love him! And to Hell with all the stupid traditions and rules."

I plopped down on the sofa and cried into my arms. Father placed a comforting hand on my back and began rubbing in circles. "There, there, Rose. I'm sorry I didn't tell you any of this sooner. And I know you feel like you are in love with Harrison, but how could that be? You haven't known each other that long. Surely, you can find yourself loving Peter, Ilya, or Phineas."

I looked up at him with wet eyes. "Peter will leave, too," I said quietly.

Father's eyes widened and he sat down next to me. "No. No, they wouldn't. That would mean allowing Frank into the top two. They wouldn't let a traitor so close to the Crown."

"Believe it, Father. They've been shunning Peter all evening and falling for Frank's charms." We both sat in companionable silence for a few moments. Shaking my head, I said, "I can't go back in there, Father. I am going to retire for the night. Go ahead and do the announcements without me. I don't think I can bear it and maintain any sense of professionalism. Just make sure Harrison comes and sees me before he leaves."

Father only nodded numbly as I stood to go. Stopping short of leaving, I looked over my shoulder to Father and said quietly, "Let us just hope that Phineas or Ilya can outdo Frank in whatever the final test is, Father." By the expression on Father's pale face, I was pretty sure I knew it was unlikely.

Chapter 19

Upon arriving to my room, I started a hot bath and got right into it. I cried at the injustice of my life, wishing that I could step back into my false one and hold Harmony close. My life with her was superior to this one in so many ways. I would gladly give up my Crown to go back. At least in that reality, there was a chance of falling in love again.

The Council's liking of Phineas rather than Harrison was understandable. Phineas was more polished and professional while Harrison was relaxed and personable.

However, the shunning of Peter was beyond me. Because his family had been an integral part of our kingdom since the beginning, I would have thought they would embrace him as a future King. The fact they seemed enraptured by Frank, of all people, was a wonder. Yes, he put on a good show for people, but everyone knew what he was: a traitor.

I pulled myself from the tub after a while and put on a cozy set of satin pajamas. Glancing at the time, I knew the party would be ending and Father would be making his announcement. Harrison would be leaving tonight. Peter would be able to, as well, and I pondered whether or not he would abandon me. I wouldn't know until the next day if Ilya or Phineas would still be there, but I had a feeling it would be Phineas.

I sat on my sofa and stared at my door for what felt like hours, although I was sure it was under even one before a knocking came to my door. I padded over to it, knowing it was Harrison on the other side. When I opened the door, I was surprised to see not only Harrison in a long wool coat with his luggage, but Peter as well.

"Harrison," I whispered. He took my hand and pulled me close and held me. For a few moments we just stood there like that, with him stroking my hair. Harrison pulled away and cupped my face in his hands.

"I am so sorry," he said.

"It's not your fault. There was nothing you could do."

"I could have been more professional. I could have been more like – like Phineas."

I shook my head and placed my small hands on top of his large ones on my face. "I love you for who you are – What am I going to do without you?"

"Fall in love with Phineas."

I closed my eyes. Phineas was chosen. Of course. "What if –" I swallowed, hardly able to say my biggest fear without bile rising in my throat. "What if Frank becomes my King?"

Harrison's brow furrowed and Peter's did the same. "I will be tracking what happens tomorrow. If Frank wins, if he tries anything traitorous, I – I –"

"There will be nothing you can do. I will have to be strong for my people."

Harrison nodded. "I'm going home tonight, too," Peter said.

"I figured you would," I said, disappointed with my friend.

"I think it's best that way," Peter said. I still wasn't looking at him.

"Fine. Go, then." Peter did as I asked, looking ashamed of himself, and left Harrison and I alone. He was still cupping my face in his hands.

"Ilya says goodbye. He couldn't bring himself to come up here himself," Harrison said.

"I understand."

"I can't kiss you goodbye, Rose. I've lost. It would be improper."

"I know," I said, letting him pull me into one more hug. "Be safe. Comm me when you make it home, alright?"

"I will. I look forward to Southland's future dealings with Arboria." Harrison pulled away, kissed my hand, and left.

Goodbye, my love.

I thought it to him. I would miss how he could know my thoughts and feelings and be there when I needed him without asking. Every so often, I had been annoyed with his mind-reading, but I realized then how fast it had become a part of my life. When I could no longer see him, I turned and went back into my room. Turning off my lights, I laid in bed staring at the canopy of my bed, glowing green from the Space Needle's light.

Shortly after getting comfortable, I heard whispers outside my door. As the voices got louder, I could tell it was Frank and Earl arguing at my door, so I got out of bed and pressed my ear to the door to listen in.

"I demand an audience with Miriam right now, Earl," Frank was saying, sounding like it was the hundredth time he had made the demand.

"No, Francis. The Crown Princess is rather upset tonight and it is well past midnight. I am positive she does not want to see you and I will not disturb her for you," Earl was explaining calmly.

"Do you understand who I am now?"

"You are still *only* a participant in the King's Test. I do not take orders from you."

"I am one step away from being King. You dare speak to me in this way?"

"I dare to do my job. Unlike you, I actually care for the Crown Princess' safety and my job is to protect her throughout the night."

"You think I would hurt her? I would never do that. She means everything to me."

I blanched at his very forthright statement to Earl. Even though I knew it to be true, it was still odd hearing him make such a declaration when I wasn't around to hear it. On second thought, he *had* already hurt me in the past, but I did know that he was unhealthily obsessed with me.

"I do not think you would hurt her physically *again*, Francis," Earl said, reminding him that he already had, "but surely you must see that a visit from you tonight of all nights would hurt her emotionally. She would take it as you mocking her for losing the one *she* loves tonight. If you want any chance of her ever falling in love with you, you have to give her time to mourn."

There was silence as I was sure Frank considered everything Earl was saying. "Very well. I'll give her tonight to mourn, but I *will* see her tomorrow."

Whatever, Frank.

While Frank's footsteps faded off into the distance, I sat and listened some more to make sure he was really gone. When I was sure he was, I opened the door and looked at Earl. "Thank you, Earl. He is the last person I want to see tonight or any night."

"Of course, Miriam," he said with an empathetic smile.

Returning his smile, I went back into my room. Allowing him to shut the door behind me, I climbed back into bed and fell asleep.

The moon is full over the clear waters of Kona. I lay in the sand in a simple black bathing suit, relishing the warm breeze that blows over me. Stars shine brightly overhead and I let my tears fall freely down the side of my face.

I miss this place. This beach. How I wish I had been able to bring David here. Is this beach still in existence? Was it destroyed when the world died and was reborn?

I miss Harrison and wish he was here with me. I feel a hand cover mine and I look over, expecting to see David. Instead, I see Harrison, laying on his side with a mischievous look in his eye.

"Harrison? Are you really here or are you a new figment of my imagination?"

Harrison laughs. "I'm really here. I've been asleep for a while now."

"How?"

"I don't know. All I can figure is that we must have some connection mentally. I felt like you called me. This must be your doing. I've never been able to read anyone as well as I can read you, Rose."

"I'm glad you're here."

"Where are we?"

"Kailua-Kona, Hawaii, as I remember it. It was my favorite place in my false life. We were on our way to the airport to fly here when David and Tom died. I was expecting to see him, not you when I turned."

"Sorry to disappoint," Harrison teases.

"You're not a disappointment. You're the happiest thing that has happened all night."

"Maybe you no longer need David, like he wanted."

I shrug. "We'll have to see if he shows up when you're not around."

Harrison places a giant hand on my cheek and sighs. "I have no idea how I will ever love again after you."

"You'll have to, or you can doom yourself to a loveless marriage like I will have."

"Phineas will be good to you. I know it."

"I don't doubt that. By the look on Father's face, though, he thinks Frank will win."

"I wonder why he thinks that."

"He doesn't tell me anything. Obviously. Or I would have told you about tonight."

Harrison and I sit up to watch the sunrise. I snuggle into him and he pulls me tightly against his side. "You'll have to wake up soon, huh?" Harrison asks.

"Yes. Adele will probably be in my room all chipper and annoying."

Harrison kisses the top of my head. "I will always love you, Rose."

I look into his eyes. "I will always love you, too."

Chapter 20

When I opened my eyes, Adele was hovering over me. It made for an odd effect because Harrison's eyes were the last thing I saw before waking up. Adele didn't say a word, but moved to let me sit up. She must have heard about Harrison going home because she wasn't as happy as she usually was.

Silently, I got out of bed and brushed my teeth. Going back into my room, I stripped from my pajamas and allowed Adele to dress me in the pale green wrap dress she selected. After putting my hair into a braided bun and doing simple makeup, she stepped away so I could step into my ivory flats and I walked out the door without saying anything. I was sure she would understand.

Wordlessly, Louis followed at his normal distance as I made my way down to the Dining Hall for breakfast. I was still furious with Father for the ridiculous deal he had made with the Council, but there was nothing that could be done at this point. I had to just accept the way things were and hope for the best.

Before going into the Dining Hall, I straightened my shoulders and tilted my chin up. I was unsurprised to find the seat between Phineas and Frank emptied. I supposed they expected me to sit between the two men, but I was in no mood to acquiesce to anyone's desires at the moment. I moved over and sat in the empty seat next to Mother and began to pick at the berries and cream in the dish in front of me.

Father cleared his throat and I looked at him with my dagger-eyes. His face read pain and regret and he silently begged my forgiveness. Coldly, I simply returned my attention to my breakfast and ignored it. He felt bad? Good. He should.

Mother took my hand. "Are you doing alright, Rose?"

I looked at her. "Did you know?"

"No, I – I had no idea." Obviously, Father must have filled her in at some point, though, because she knew exactly what I was talking about.

"Good. At least I have one parent I can depend on." I took a bite, again ignoring the painful expression on Father's face. All this was his fault. He was too weak to deny the Council's demands. He cared more about the tradition of the King's Test than allowing his daughter to marry the man she loved.

"Rose –" Mother begged.

"When will the wedding dress be ready for a fitting? I am excited to see what Mr. Tailor has put together for me. I trust Adele is still working with him?" I said all this with a thick layer of false sweetness, adding to the chagrined expression on Father's face.

Sighing, Mother gave up her plea for Father and answered my question. "It should be ready for a fitting tomorrow. He will also do a final fitting for whichever man ends up winning the King's Test. You will both be present for it."

I silently wondered if it was no longer considered bad luck for the groom to see the wedding dress, but could say nothing because Phineas did not know my secret.

"You know, before the Daze, it was considered bad luck for the groom to see the wedding gown before the wedding," Frank said with a momentary glace in my direction. I had no idea why he had that piece of trivia locked away, but was grateful for the way he answered the question he knew I was probably thinking.

"Ah. Superstitions. I am glad we no longer think such a thing. I am sure Miriam will be a sight to behold in her gown," Phineas said.

Frank shot him a look. "I am sure she will be."

We all ate in silence for a while before Father finally spoke up. "After breakfast, Phineas and Francis will head up to Doctor Bartholomew's office for the final test. It is a written exam on the history, culture, and traditions of Arboria."

I sighed and crushed my eyes closed. *That* was why he thought Frank was going to win. Having been born and raised in Arboria, he clearly had an advantage in the test. Considering the fact that this King's Test was originally intended for foreign Princes only, it made sense that he would want the one to win to be most knowledgeable about our kingdom.

Pushing away my dish and rolling my eyes open, I said, "I am no longer hungry. When will you be announcing the winner, Father?"

"At dinner tonight at 5:00," he grumbled.

"Alright. I am going to go back to bed now. I had a long night and have not had opportunity for good sleep lately."

As I stood, Frank spoke up, "Sir, might I request permission to escort the Crown Princess to her room?"

I looked at Father, hoping he would have the common sense to not anger me further. "Go ahead, Francis. When you are finished, please go directly to the testing room." I pursed my lips and tried to make my glare even angrier, though I was not sure if I succeeded. With a quick step, I took off out the door, Frank jogging to keep up.

"Miriam, wait up!" Frank said as he caught up with me at the Core and grabbed my hand.

"What is it, Frank? Why can't you just leave me be?" I continued walking, though I slowed down because Frank wouldn't allow me to tug him any faster than he wanted to go.

"Why can't I – Seriously, Miriam? You know why I can't leave you be."

"Enlighten me," I said without slowing down or making eye contact with the gremlin.

"I – I would rather have this conversation in private," he said softly.

"Fine. Then hurry up."

At my demand, he did hurry up – he ended up in front of me and pulled me into my room. Louis gave me an asking look and I simply rolled my eyes to let him know I was not afraid. Frank pressed the button to close the door behind us, then pressed me against the door with his weight.

"What are you doing, Frank? This is very inappropriate and you *know* Louis is right outside the door. I thought you wanted privacy." I shoved him away and walked passed him.

Frank grabbed my hand again and pressed me against the wall. "You know this game, Miriam. It is not difficult for me to trap you at all."

"Is that what this is? Are you trying to make me your captive again?"

"I am *trying* to make you my wife. Based on the topic of the test, it seems that you *will* be, so get used to this." His words were harsh, but his voice was soft with desire, and he whispered them in my ear. "I do not want this. I do not want to fight with you. I want to love you. I want to cherish you and hold you. I want to kiss you until I can no longer breathe and share my bed with you. Can't you see? I still love you. I have never stopped."

"I can see that, Frank. But you still scare me," I whispered. The way he had me against the wall, I was forced to look into his eyes. "Please, show some self-restraint." I was trembling, not because I feared *Frank*, but because I feared a marriage to him.

"You're shaking. You really are still afraid of me." Frank slowly released me from the prison of his body against mine. "Alright, Miriam. I will restrain myself on one condition."

"You have conditional restraint?"

"When it comes to you, yes."

I considered him for a moment, then nodded.

"I will not kiss you or ask anything of you until I am declared your betrothed tonight at dinner. When we are engaged, will you allow me to kiss you?"

I didn't want to agree to his condition, but the alternative would probably mean more of his attentions right then. "I *could* just scream and Louis would come in here to escort you out."

"He would, but it would not change things, Miriam. One way or another, you will have to get used to me. You will have to bed with me to produce an heir to the Crown. You will have to rule with me by your side."

"Only if you get a higher score on the exam than Phineas."

Frank scoffed. "You think a *foreigner* is going to score higher than me on this exam?" I could have sworn the f-bomb was implied in the way he said 'foreigner.' "He has been here for months while I have been here my whole life. It would be a travesty if he scored higher."

"It is still possible," I whispered, reaching over and tracing the bark on one of the trees in my room.

Frank took a step towards me and I pressed myself against the wall as I pulled my hand back, remembering for a moment that he did the same thing to me over and over again while he had me in captivity. He stopped and put his hands out in front of him. "Then you shouldn't have a problem meeting my condition."

Heaving a deep sigh and hoping for the best, I said, "Alright. I will allow you to kiss me *if* you are declared the winner of the King's Test."

"If I become your betrothed?"

"Isn't it the same thing?"

"I like the wording better. I told you before, I will never consider you a prize to be won."

"Very well. I will allow you to kiss me *if* you become my betrothed."

Smiling at his victory, he nodded once and left to take his test.

Chapter 21

As much as I wanted to just go back to bed, I couldn't, especially not after the promise I had just made to Frank. After a couple hours of lying in bed, trying to sleep, I gave up and left my room. Louis and I didn't speak often, but I needed someone to talk to and he was the only one available that I trusted.

"Walk with me down to the rose garden, Louis," I said.

"That is my job, Your Crowned Highness," Louis responded formally.

Making our way down the Core, I kept our usual quiet. When he stationed himself outside the garden, I said, "No. Please join me. I need someone to talk to."

Louis quirked a brow at me. "You want to talk with me?"

I looked him in the eyes, feeling utterly alone. "Please, Louis. I have no one left that I can trust completely."

With a defeated sigh, Louis opened the door to the garden and followed me in. To keep things proper, I sat on a regular wooden bench on the outskirts of the maze and gestured for Louis to join me. "Is everything alright, Miriam?"

"No."

Louis rubbed the back of his neck, clearly unsure how he felt about the situation I had put him in. "That was a stupid question. I am sorry."

I laughed dryly. "No, it was an opening question. It is quite alright." I sighed. "I just cannot believe my misfortune, Louis. How can that traitor be so close to the Crown and to me?"

His jaw clenched. "It is maddening for all of us loyal to the Royal family, Miriam; those of us in the Guard, in particular."

"What am I going to do if he wins?" I was no longer looking at him, moving my gaze to the glass wall. I knew he was only there as a sounding board and I didn't want him feeling any more uncomfortable than he already was. "He will have everything he wanted in the first place. He will be King and he will be my husband. He will have me and I will have to be – intimate with him. How can anyone expect for me to produce an heir to the Crown of Arboria with *him*?"

He shifted in his seat and frowned at the awkward turn in the conversation and was quietly thoughtful for a bit. "I cannot protect you from *that*, Miriam, but I can tell you that I will not let any harm come to you. I swear to you that I will feign loyalty to Frank, if it comes to it, just to keep you safe."

My mouth dropped. "I am touched by the offer, Louis, but you have a family to think of. If Frank becomes King, Evergreen Palace will become a dangerous place to be. I am not sure I can allow it."

"Please, accept my offer. I could not return home to my family, safe and sound, and feel good about leaving you in danger."

I swallowed hard, moved by Louis' loyalty. "Very well. I accept your vow. Thank you, Louis."

"I will leave you to your thoughts now and take my post outside," he said, desiring an escape, I thought.

Obliging, I said, "Thank you, Louis." When he left, I got up and moved to the center of the maze to sit in the sofa swing and watch the storm rage overhead. I did not concern myself with time; when it was time for dinner and the announcement, I knew Louis would come get me.

Stretching out so I was lying on my back, I thought about Frank and how I would deal with whatever he dished out if or when we were married. One thing was certain: the time I was currently taking for myself would have to be the end of my moping if I was ever going to be considered a strong and worthy Queen.

If we were wed, I would not allow myself to become his doormat. Nor would I allow myself to be pushed around by the Arborian Council the way Father had been. No, I wouldn't become a tyrant. But what point was there to have a King and Queen if we were nothing more than pretty faces to print on our currency?

As difficult as it was, I needed to let go of my false life completely and embrace this real one. David, Tom, and Harmony were not real and never had been. Being Crown Princess meant I needed to be competent and ready. I could wish my false life was real all day long and it would make no difference to reality.

"Miriam?"

I looked over to see Phineas standing in the archway, but I didn't stand or even sit up. "Hello, Phineas. I am sorry you had to witness my wrath this morning. I have taken my time to recuperate and am in much better control of my attitude now."

Phineas looked down at his entwined fingers. "Phin."

"Pardon?" I asked, finally looking at him.

"Call me Phin, Miriam."

"Oh. Alright."

He smiled as he came and sat by me on the edge of the sofa. "I think I did it, Miriam."

"Did what?"

Phin met my eyes with an excited twinkle in his. "I think I got a perfect score on the exam. In fact, Frank was still working on his when I left a little over a half hour ago."

That got me to sit up, which brought my face very close to his. "You think you got a perfect score?" Phin nodded excitedly. "How sure are you?"

The answer to my question came in the form of Phin pulling me taut against him and kissing me breathlessly. He had been telling me all along that he would only kiss me if I was to become his wife. If he was certain enough of his results to kiss me, it made me certain as well. Relief flooded my senses and while I wasn't in love with Phin I gripped him close and returned his kiss.

He pulled away, then kissed my cheek. "I know you are not in love with me yet, Miriam, but I swear this to you. I will be good to you and prove myself worthy of your love every day for the rest of our lives." As I nodded numbly, Phin stood up and started to go.

"Phin!" I yelled after him and he turned around. "Rose. Call me Rose." His smile widened and he left the maze.

After he was gone, it hit me that I had just counted my apples before they ripened. Then it hit me that I remembered slang from my current time that had never been mentioned to me before. I smiled, not caring about Phin and my premature celebration. He wasn't Harrison, but he wasn't Frank either, and *that* was something.

Chapter 22

By the time dinner rolled around, I was nervous again. Phin was so sure of his score, but who was to say that Frank didn't get a perfect score, too – or if Phin really *did* get a perfect score. I walked into the Dining Hall in the same way I had that morning, shoulders back and chin up. No emotion crossed my face as I realized the entire Arborian Council was present for the announcement.

There were three seats at a smaller table stationed on a wooden stage – eerily similar to the one in my vision – that had been set up in front of everyone. Phin sat in the right chair and Frank sat on the left. Assuming the center chair was for me, I walked straight to it, not stopping to greet Father or Mother, and took my seat.

Everyone was still conversing at the lower table, and picking at appetizer plates scattered all over it. Taking a shrimp roll and popping it into my mouth, I was grateful that the food at the palace was good. If everything else went south that night, at least there was that.

Frank bent over and whispered into my ear as he gently grabbed my knee, "I'm looking forward to sharing that kiss with you tonight, Miriam. I'm feeling really good about the exam. I certainly took more time to complete it than Phineas did."

Pushing his hand off my lap and pulling away slightly, I whispered back the slang I had remembered earlier. "Don't count your apples before they've ripened, Frank. Phin – eas still has a chance."

Frank shrugged, then laughed heartily at my statement. "I'll be weeded by the roots if that foreigner scored higher than me."

"Is that a promise?" I asked with a demure smile.

Frank blanched at my forwardness. "Why, Miriam. Have you gone and gained some confidence over the last few hours?"

I patted his cheek playfully. "Let's just say that if I am forced to marry you, I won't be a docile kitten for you to control. I have claws and I intend on using them."

I turned over to Phin, who was trying desperately not to laugh at how terrified Frank looked, and gave him a genuine smile. Bending over to him, I gave him a kiss on the cheek and Frank clenched his jaw with a frown.

Dinner was served and it was unnerving to me how all the people present, besides the three of us on stage, were able to carry on as if my future and the future of our kingdom wasn't on the line.

Because of his role in the final test, Doctor Bartholomew was present and seated next to Father. I still had no idea if Bartholomew was his first or last name. Perhaps I had never known to begin with. When the tables were cleared and the wine was poured, Doctor Bartholomew passed an envelope over to Father, who took a deep breath.

Without opening the envelope, Father stood and cleared his throat to gain everyone's attention. "Ladies and gentlemen, thank you for joining my family and the remaining participants of the King's Test for this dinner and most important announcement.

"This generation's King's Test has been riddled with one complication after another, but a future King has finally been decided through a series of both subjective and objective tests. The two men before you are the only remnants of a beginning group of twenty: ten Arborians and ten Princes.

"They have proven themselves over this last week in multiple ways and soon, when I open this envelope and read what is within it, one will be declared not only the future King of Arboria, but the future husband of my daughter, Crown Princess Miriam Petrichoria.

"Because of recent events, not only was the King's Test shortened drastically, but the engagement will be as well. Saturday at 1:00 in the afternoon, the future Crown Prince will wed Crown Princess Miriam. After the wedding, the Crowning Coronation for the Crown Prince will occur.

"Before I read the results, let us drink to the future of Arboria," Father said, raising his glass.

"To the future of Arboria," we all repeated and sipped our wine.

Setting down his glass, Father opened the envelope and pulled out a slip of paper. Nodding, he replaced the paper and turned to face the three of us. Phin quietly reached over and held my hand, entwining his fingers with mine. I smiled at him.

"Phin, Frank. You have both performed admirably in the King's Test, but only one of you can become King and Crown Princess Miriam's husband. This final exam was difficult on purpose. It is important that the future King of this kingdom is knowledgeable about its people and its history. One of you scored perfectly."

Frank smiled menacingly and Phin smiled excitedly. At that moment, I knew both of them thought they had scored perfectly and I was suddenly nervous.

"The other missed only one question. But that was enough for there to be one clear winner."

With that declaration, both men's smiles faltered and I felt sweat begin to drip down the side of my face.

"The man who will become the King of Arboria is – Prince Phineas of Britainnia!"

Phin smiled and jumped out of his seat, pulling me up and spinning me in a circle. I held on to his shoulders tightly, afraid that he would drop me, but he didn't. As everyone applauded, he kissed me soundly.

Our kiss was interrupted by Frank throwing his chair across the room and storming out of the Dining Hall. When he left, the chatter resumed and Phin kissed me again. "You have made me the happiest man. I promise, I will make you the happiest woman."

Part III

Chapter 23

Closing my eyes, I leaned against my door. Adele was waiting for me on my sofa, but said nothing as she got up and began getting my bath ready for me. Phin had escorted me back to my room, thrilled that we would be getting married in only a few short days.

While I was glad that, by some miracle, Phin had beaten out Frank on an exam about Arboria, I didn't love him. It was good to know that he loved me and there was always the possibility that my affinity for him could eventually turn into love. However, my heart still belonged to Harrison.

On the one hand, I hoped to see Harrison again when I dreamed that night. On the other, I knew that if he continued to visit me, I would never get over him. That wouldn't be fair for Phin, and I wouldn't feel right essentially seeing someone behind his back. With that understanding, I knew my long day wouldn't end if I fell asleep and found Harrison.

Another bit of knowledge I got was that Phin's brother, *King George XV* would be coming into Arboria the day before our wedding. Apparently after the debacle about the King's Test ten years ago, he ended up finding a bride in Prince Leonardo's sister, Domonique. I was certainly not looking forward to that awkward reunion.

"Your bath is ready, Miriam. Would you like me to stay until you are finished or would you like to be alone?" Adele asked.

Opening my eyes and meeting her gaze, I said, "I would like to be alone tonight, I think. Thank you. Please let Earl know I do not wish to see anyone tonight."

"Very well," Adele said. I moved away from the door so she could leave and she placed a hand on my shoulder. "Everything will be fine, Miriam. I am sure of it."

"Thank you, Adele."

After she left, I got out of my clothing. Because of all the late nights I had been having, I had gotten quite adept at removing my own corsets. I sank myself into the sweet-smelling bath and allowed all my muscles to relax and soak in the heat and oils.

The way Frank had left was concerning to me, especially not knowing where he went when he exited the palace grounds. I knew he would be upset if he lost, but I didn't realize *how* upset he would be. Even though he publicly made an order that his followers would need to respect whoever won the King's Test, I wondered if they would.

If there were riots, the Royal Arborian Guard would just need to take care of it. I had every confidence that they could handle Frank's unruly supporters. I was just glad that Frank was no longer at Evergreen Palace. No longer would I need to fear turning into him in the hallway or being forced to marry him in a couple days. He was gone.

I pulled myself out of the tub and dried off using one of my over-large towels. Slipping into my pajamas, I crawled into my bed and shut off my lights. I fell asleep before I even finished curling into a ball.

I am back in the Dining Hall, dressed in what I was wearing earlier in the evening. Rather than tables and chairs, a sofa swing hangs in the middle of the room and Harrison sits on it, waiting for me.

"So, who's the lucky man?" he asks me.

I walk over and snuggle into him. "Phin."

"Phin?"

"Yes. Frank lost. He was really upset. He threw his chair across the room before storming out."

"No. I mean, you're calling him 'Phin' now?"

"Oh... Yes. That's what he asked me to call him."

"Huh."

We swing in companionable quiet, neither one of us saying what was on our minds.

"Did he kiss you?" Harrison asks sadly.

"Yes. He says he loves me."

"Good."

I laugh sadly. "You don't have to be all noble. It's alright to be upset. I am."

"At least it's not Frank. I don't think I could stand that. Phineas at least seems to be a good man."

"Seems to be?"

Harrison shrugs. "You never really know what people are like until there's nothing left for them to gain or lose by you. I suppose we'll see what he's really like after you're married."

"I suppose." It is the perfect segway to tell him we can't see each other like this anymore. Taking a deep breath, I say, "Harrison, we need to talk about something important."

"Hair."

"What?"

"Call me Hair," Harrison says with a straight face.

"No. I'm not going to call you Hair. That's ridiculous." I laugh.

He shrugs. "Everyone else seems to be shortening their name. Seems like the fashionable thing to do."

When I laugh even harder, he can't hold it back anymore and we laugh together. We finally calm down and take another deep breath, ready to try again.

"Harrison?"

"I know. We need to talk." He traces invisible patterns on my arm. "I knew we would if Frank didn't come out on top."

Sitting up, I turn his face so he's looking at me. "We can't do this anymore."

He sighs. "I know."

"It's not fair or right to do to Phin."

"I know."

"Will you kiss me this time? One last time?"

"No."

"I figured you would say that." I put my palm on his cheek. *"You're a good man, Harrison. I'll miss you."*

"I'll miss you, too."

Chapter 24

"Rise and shine, Miriam," Adele said, waking me up. When I opened my eyes, I was greeted with green light.

"It is still dark outside. It cannot possibly be time to wake up," I whine.

Adele rips the blankets off my body and I shiver in the coolness of the early morning. "It is, indeed, time to wake up. The King has called an emergency meeting with you, the Queen, Prince Phineas, and High General Miller and I need to get you ready."

"An emergency meeting? Is there even such a thing as a normal night's sleep here? I used to complain about 6:30 AM. Now, I would be happy for it. It would be like sleeping in."

Adele laughed. "Things have been unusual since your return. Things should calm down in time. Put these on." She handed me some white trousers and a brown blouse. Grumbling to myself, I got out of bed and changed into the new clothes, grateful that I was at least getting to wear pants for once.

"Do you know what the meeting is about?" I asked her.

"Top secret. I do not know anything except that I need to get you up and out of bed."

After a few minutes, someone knocked on my door and Adele went over to answer it. "Oh. Good morning, Prince Phineas. I was not expecting you this morning."

"Phin?"

I turned around to see him, slightly embarrassed at my appearance and the smile that came to his face when he saw my half-completed face and puffy pillow hair. "So, this is what I will be waking up to every morning," Phin said with a teasing smile.

"Very funny, Phin. What you'll see every morning is worse than what you see now."

"I don't see how that can be," he laughed.

I dropped my jaw in mock surprise. "Phin! Did you just use a contraction with me?"

"I certainly did." Phin walked over and kissed my cheek.

"What are you doing here? I'm not nearly ready yet."

"You are nearly ready," piped in Adele as she walked over and continued working on my face. Phin leaned over her shoulder and began to watch her work. She paused. "Prince Phineas, with all due respect, I need you to stop hovering, so I can make your fiancée presentable."

"Alright, alright." Phin laughed and plopped himself on my sofa.

"Make yourself right at home, Phin," I mumbled sarcastically.

"I will." He kicked his feet up on my coffee table and leaned back, his arms folded behind his head. He had never been so comfortable with me and I liked the change. "Do you have any idea what this meeting is about, Rose?" Phin asked.

"I was going to ask you. I don't have any idea," I replied. Adele finished with my makeup and moved on to my hair. She was quick with her work, but good. It was one of the things I liked so much about her.

"What do you think, Prince Phineas? Shall I put her hair up or down today?" Adele surprisingly asked Phin.

"Hey! You never ask for *my* opinion!" I protested.

"Shush, Miriam," she scolded. "What do you think, Prince Phineas?"

"Did you just 'shush' her?" he asked with an amused grin.

"Yes, I did."

"I like her, Rose."

"Shush, Phin. Give the lady your opinion," I said.

He chuckled. "Down. I like it that way."

"Noted," Adele said as she brushed it. When she finished, she placed my tiara on my head and took her leave.

Once she was gone, I went over and helped Phin stand from my cushy sofa. Facing me, he ran his fingers through the full length of my long hair. "Perfect," he said and I felt heat rise into my cheeks. He kissed one, then took my hand. "Let's go, Rose."

Louis followed behind us at an appropriate distance as we made our way down the Core and to Father's office. When we got there, I noticed Father, Mother, and High General Miller were already there and seated. No one else was in the room, which was odd. Usually,

Father had at least one maid or butler available for bringing coffee or assisting in other ways.

Phin and I sat down on a sofa together, still holding hands. "What is going on, Father?"

"We have lost contact with the Willow Province on the coast," he said.

"What do you mean 'lost contact?'"

"There has been no communication originating there and there have been no responses to messages sent from here."

"That *is* strange. How long has it been that way?"

"Since around midnight."

I looked at High General Miller out of the corner of my eye, then back to Father. "What do you think happened?"

"I think you know," Father said.

I did know. Willow province was where that blasted island was – the one Frank held me captive on. Just the thought of the corner of that horrid cell caused me to begin hyperventilating.

Phin squeezed my hand to help calm me, but it didn't work. "Frank," I breathed. "But – he said that he and his followers would respect the outcome of the King's Test. He said –"

"It does not matter what he said. We have been monitoring the island off the Willow Coast and there have been 'fishing boats' arriving all morning."

"Well, why is it just us meeting? Should we not have a meeting of the Council?"

"I do not trust them right now."

"Why not?"

"If the Willow Nobles and Delegate were trustworthy, do you not think they would have responded to me by now?"

"I suppose, but –"

"If there is even a possibility that their loyalty has been compromised, there is a possibility *all* the provinces have been compromised."

"Have we been able to communicate with the other provinces?" Phin asked. I noticed that he had said "we" and it was a comfort to know he already considered himself one of us.

"Yes. All the other provinces have been responsive," Father responded.

I sighed. "With all due respect, is there a purpose for the High General being here this morning? I am not convinced he has not sided with his son and it seems unwise to have him here."

"Miriam!" Mother said.

"No. I understand the Crown Princess' concern," High General Miller said. "I am loyal to this kingdom and its Royal family. I am here to make suggestions on how to proceed."

I let go of Phin's hand and leaned forward. "How is it that your son turned out to become the biggest traitor in our kingdom's history if you are so loyal, High General?"

Mother's face paled, but Father seemed to be considering my words.

"I do not understand how he turned out the way he did. I have taught him the ways of our people and tried to instill a sense of nationalism in him, but, apparently, I failed. Now, I feel it is my responsibility to clean up the mess I have made with my mistakes."

I nodded, though I still wasn't completely convinced. Sitting back up, I asked, "What actions do you think we should take, High General Miller?"

"I think we should bring more of the Guard to Evergreen Palace and double the personal Guards of the Royal family, including Prince Phineas."

"I agree with the High General, Father," I said, turning to address him again.

"I do, too." Father turned to Mother. "Amoura, you and Rose should head up to the Dining Hall and we will stay here and figure out numbers and such."

I glanced at Phin, who seemed to understand that his job was starting even before the wedding.

"Alright. Phineas, we will see you later at the fitting at 10:00. Meet us in Miriam's room," Mother said.

Phin nodded. I gave him a kiss on the cheek before standing and leaving with Mother.

Chapter 25

Mother and I began breakfast in relative silence. With everything that had been going on lately, there had not been much time for us to spend together. Knowing the wedding was only two days away, I figured we were about to spend a lot of time together.

"I – uh – I'm not really sure how weddings work nowadays. Can you tell me about them?" I asked.

"Why don't you tell me about your wedding with David and I will let you know about the differences?" Mother answered my question with a question.

"Well, our wedding was a little different than a normal wedding because we already had Tom."

"You already had a child *before* you were married?" Mother asked with disapproval in her voice.

"Yes. It wasn't something we were proud of – getting pregnant out of wedlock, but we loved Tom and decided to include him in the ceremony. On top of the regular wedding vows to each other, we made familial vows with Tom.

"Logistically, I had a Maid of Honor and two Bridesmaids while David had a Best Man and two Groomsmen. During the ceremony, they all stood up on a stage with us as special witnesses. David's Best Man and Groomsmen escorted my Maid of Honor and Bridesmaids before Tom walked me down the aisle. Tom walked with me because my parents were dead in my false life. Else, it would have been my dad that walked me down."

"For your wedding with Phin," Mother began, "His brother and sister-in-law will stand with him at the altar, while Father and I walk you to it and we will stand with you. The Pastor will conduct the ceremony, which will include an explanation of why we will be gathered, an exchange of rings and vows, and a pronouncement of your being wed."

"The second part is pretty similar to what I would expect. What about decorations? We had flowers and ribbon in the sanctuary and reception hall in coordinating colors with the outfits worn by the wedding party."

"The sanctuary will be left as it is, but the Main Ballroom, where your reception will be, will be adorned with red and ivory roses, rubies, and diamonds. We picked everything out many years ago together, so it is simply a matter of finding similar things to what we selected and making sure everything gets done."

We sat in silence again for a few more minutes before I broke it. "I cannot believe I am getting married again in two days. Everything seems to be moving so fast."

Mother took my hand, "I know life seems to be going fast, Rose, but things will calm down after Phineas' Crowning Coronation."

"Adele said something like that earlier," I muttered.

"Well, she is right."

I nodded, but didn't respond to her. After another moment, Mother asked, "Have you told Phineas yet?"

I tugged on a loose thread in my napkin and asked casually, "Told him what?"

"Rose. You know what I mean."

I did. I knew what she meant. "No. I haven't told him about my memory yet. I'm too afraid."

"Afraid of what, dear? He's going to be your husband."

"I know. And he's been nothing but kind and wonderful to me, but – I don't know. Something is off about things right now. I just can't put my finger on it."

"He will need to know eventually."

"I understand."

Mother and I finished eating, then stood and walked over to the windows to watch the rain pour onto the field behind the palace. The wildflowers that had been there when I woke up from my freeze were no longer in bloom and the water was falling so hard, small ponds began to form all over.

When Father and Phin came into the Dining Hall, Father escorted Mother from the room and Phin came over to stand behind me. Wrapping his arms around my waist, he rested his chin on my shoulder and watched the rain with me for a while. "Rose, would you walk with me before we become living dolls in a bit?" he asked.

I smiled at the mental picture he created. "Yes," I said, turning around so I was facing him. "Let's get umbrellas and walk in the rain."

Smiling, Phin ran his fingers through my hair. "Adele will kill me if I ruin your beautiful hair."

"No, she won't. She knows that there is no fighting me when I want something bad enough." I smiled mischievously and he slouched his shoulders in mock resignation.

"Very well," Phin yielded to me. Laughing lightly, I took his hand in mine and led us down the Core. Grabbing a big umbrella as we exited the building, I opened it and handed it over to Phin. Louis and three new Guards followed behind us and I was glad for the extra security.

It had been too long since I left Evergreen Palace. I hadn't even left the grounds since waking up several months ago. I nodded to one of the Guards at the gate and he let us through.

Bright lights illuminated every storefront on the street and people waved to us as we strolled by. I wasn't sure when Father had made the announcement to the public about our engagement, but he clearly had. A few people on the street said quick "congratulations" to us as they passed us.

I was glad that no one stopped and asked for autographs or pictures, but then I wondered if people even still did that. The thought sobered me and made it difficult to keep my smile on my face as we turned and made our way back to Evergreen Palace on the opposite side of the road.

"Crown Princess Miriam?"

A tiny voice interrupted my thoughts and I looked down to a girl holding flowers she had clearly picked from someone's garden.

"Hello," I lowered myself to a prim squat and smiled at her. "How are you this fine, rainy day?"

She giggled. "I am good. I picked these for you." She handed me the bunch of flowers, dirty roots still attached to the ends.

"Oh! Thank you! What is your name?" I said, sniffing the flowers.

"Rose. My daddy and mommy named me after you." I looked up at Phin, who had a Cheshire Cat smile on his face.

"It *is* a beautiful flower."

"Are you getting married to *him* tomorrow?" Rose asked with widened eyes now looking at Phin.

"I am marrying *him*, but on Saturday, not tomorrow."

She leaned forward and whispered loudly in my ear, "He is *awful* handsome."

"He sure is." I stood up and kissed him on the cheek, which sent little Rose into another fit of giggles and Phin's cheeks reddened. "Thank you for the flowers," I said as we continued on our way.

Phin and I walked in amiable silence until we made it through the gates to the palace again. Quietly, I said, "I need to talk to you about something important, Phin."

Stopping me, he looked into my eyes. "You can tell me anything, Rose."

I swallowed hard. "After the fitting. It needs to be in private."

He nodded and we made our way into the palace and up the Core to my room, where Mother was waiting with Mr. Tailor. After the fitting, I would be letting yet another person know the secret that could destroy me.

Chapter 26

It took three women to get me into my wedding dress. If anything horrible happened on my wedding day, I would be royally rotten. The skirt had a circumference of at least four feet and I could barely breathe in my corset.

Don't get me wrong – the dress was gorgeous. Braedon Tailor definitely knew what he was doing. The tight bodice had a pattern of vines and rubies carved like roses embroidered on it. I couldn't tell how long the train actually was because it was longer than the length of my room. The white skirt was overlaid with soft lace.

When I stepped out of the bathroom, everyone was focused on Phin in his white tuxedo. Unlike the tuxedos I was used to seeing, the jacket of his had tails. Beneath his jacket was a forest green vest and tucked in the breast pocket of his jacket was a forest green handkerchief. He was breathtakingly handsome.

I cleared my throat and everyone turned to look at me – it was slightly unnerving. Mr. Tailor looked proud. Mother began crying. And Phin – Phin looked terrified, which seemed odd to me.

"Goodness, Rose. You're stunning," Phin said as he stepped down off his stool and walked over to me as if in a trance. Mr. Tailor mumbled something about Phin needing to remove his tuxedo since he was done with him, but Phin didn't hear him.

"Please step up onto the stool, Your Crowned Highness," Mr. Tailor said. Phin took one of my hands and walked me over to the stool he had been standing on, then gave me both hands to help me up onto the stool. After I was on there, Mr. Tailor began fussing over the bodice and Phin left the room, with two of Mr. Tailor's assistants in tow, to remove his tuxedo.

"Mr. Tailor, I am concerned about the lack of my ability to move quickly in this gown," I said bluntly.

Mr. Tailor waved a hand of dismissal. "Psh. You will not need to move much during the ceremony and I know Adele has picked something spectacular for you for the reception that will allow for more movement. For the ceremony, all that matters is that you are gorgeous – and you are."

Mother was no help – she just nodded in agreement.

Thanks for the support, Mother.

For the next several minutes, Mr. Tailor circled me and stuck several pins all over the dress. I wasn't sure what he was marking – the dress seemed perfect to me. After he stuck the dress roughly a million times, I was sent back into the bathroom with the same three assistants that helped before.

When I was out of the dress, they left me to put my regular clothes back on. Bending over to get my trousers back on, I mentally cursed the corset trend.

Really. Why do I need to wear a corset under a shirt?

Reentering my room, I noticed everyone was gone – except Phin, who was patiently sitting on the sofa back in his earlier outfit as well. Deep in thought, he didn't notice me until I sat next to him, curling my legs beneath me.

"Oh. Sorry, Rose. I didn't hear you come in," he said quietly as he took in my close proximity to him. He had a strange look on his face – if I didn't know any better, I would have called it "guilt," but what could he possibly have to feel guilty for?

"That's alright, Phin. It has been a long day," I responded, bending over to pick up a small cube of cheese on a platter that had been brought in earlier. The fitting went well-past lunch, so food was brought to us. After taking the bite and swallowing, I noticed he was still looking at me. "Is everything alright?" I asked.

"How is it that you are even beautiful when you eat?" Phin asked. I snorted and he smiled then. Taking my hand, he said, "You told me you had something you needed to discuss with me."

"Right," I said, looking down at our entwined fingers. This man was going to be my husband and deserved to know about my problem. "What I am about to tell you is completely confidential. Only a handful of people know."

He swallowed. "Are you sure you want to tell me?"

I looked back to him. "Yes. You're going to be my husband. This is definitely information you should be aware of." He nodded for me to continue and squeezed my hand. "When I woke up from my freeze, I – I didn't come back whole."

His eyes raked by body as if he was trying to figure out what was missing and I laughed breathily. "No. I have all my body parts. Don't worry about that." Phin smirked. "My mind is – incomplete. When I woke up, I remembered a life I never had that included a late husband, dead son, and a beautiful daughter. However, I remembered nothing from this life, my real life.

"Over time, I have gotten snippets of memories at random times. For example, when Ella died, I got all my memories of her and everything that went with it. I have also had a couple memories of Peter. But I have been faking a knowledge I really don't have all this time."

Phin looked at me like I had two heads, but didn't let go of me. "You don't remember life as the Princess of this kingdom?"

"Not completely, no."

"Do they think you will get your full memory back?"

"Doctor Quincy is not sure. I guess this is the first documented time it has happened. Though, with my recent rememberings, I would think they eventually will."

Phin placed his free hand on my cheek and turned to face me. "You have hidden this from everyone?"

"Not *everyone*. But most people, yes."

Phin gently pulled me into an embrace and held me for a while. I wasn't sure if he was comforting himself or me, but we stayed that way for some time. After a while, he leaned back against the arm of the sofa and stretched out, pulling me with him so I was lying next to him and we cuddled.

As he traced his fingers along my arm, I thought about how marrying him wouldn't be so bad. He hadn't given any real response to my news, but the fact he didn't run off screaming or tell everyone he knew immediately said something for his character.

There was also the fact that in all the time I knew him, he hadn't once taken advantage of me any time we were alone. At that moment, he could have done anything with me. What he chose was to embrace and comfort me, to let me know he was there for me.

Not moving from my spot, I said, "Phin?"

"Yes, Rose?" Phin said to the ceiling.

"Are you alright? I know this isn't what you signed up for."

"I'm fine, Rose. I'm just concerned for you is all. It changes nothing about my plans. I only hope that your memory returns to you soon."

"Me, too."

When dinner time rolled around, I commed down to the kitchen and asked that it be brought up to my room. Exchanging the old lunch plates for the new dinner plates, the kitchen staff worked quickly and wordlessly.

Phin finally opened up and began asking a thousand questions about my past – both about my false life and the real life memories I had retrieved. I told him about David and my children. He wanted to know everything and I held nothing back.

Oddly enough, talking about them didn't make me cry. It was the first time I was able to talk about my false life without feeling so emotionally attached to it.

What *did* make me cry were my memories about Ella. How I wished she was still with me for my wedding day. How I wished I hadn't been so jealous. How I regretted not remembering her until she was gone. I really didn't know what I had until she was gone.

After we finished with dinner, we resumed our comfortable position of lying down on the sofa together. I appreciated that he didn't push me into anything intimate, knowing that I wasn't in love yet. When midnight came and went, Phin stood up, kissed me on the head and whispered me a good night.

I was too comfortable to get up after he was gone, so I fell asleep curled up on the sofa, glad that things were going so well and hoping they would stay that way.

Chapter 27

I stand in my parents' room looking out the window. It is my room now, though I wish it wasn't. I fear the man who will be coming soon, not knowing what to expect. Am I next? He really doesn't need me anymore now that he has what he wants.

A tear escapes my eye and I wish someone would save me – would save my kingdom. I have failed. Even with the premonitions, I have failed and I feel helpless to do anything.

I gasped and shook as I woke up from the terrible dream – vision – whatever it was. Jumping off the sofa, I quickly changed from the clothes I had been wearing the previous day into the first dress I found. I didn't even pay attention to its color.

I was sure my face and hair was a mess, but I had to see Father. Adele hadn't yet arrived, so my current appearance would have to do.

After crossing the hall, I banged on my parents' door like a maniac. The Guards looked at me like I was crazy, I probably was a little bit, but that didn't interrupt me. I had to tell them everything. About my returning memories and the visions. They had to know.

Father opened his door and widened his eyes at my appearance. "Come in, Rose."

Entering his room and having a seat on the sofa next to Mother, I twiddled my fingers nervously and my eyes darted around the room. I couldn't fail. I had to tell them.

"I need to talk to you about something," I muttered.

"Clearly," Mother said with a concerned look on her face.

"First, I have started having memories return."

"What?" Mother whispered as Father sat on the chair next to me. "I knew about the one of King George, but how long has this been happening?"

Habitually, I brought my thumb nail to my teeth and began nibbling. "Since the King's Test began. I remembered a conversation with Phin's brother while talking with him. When Ella died, I got all my memories of her and I have been getting snippets of Peter and I, as well."

"Why didn't you tell me you were getting more?" Father asked.

"More? How didn't I hear about this at all?" Mother asked.

"Sorry, dear," Father said sheepishly.

"Me, too, Mother. It's just that you had so much going on. I am still not sure if my entire memory is going to come back and I didn't want you getting your hopes up."

"You can tell us anything, Rose," Mother said.

"Good. Because there's more." I took a deep breath. "I have been having visions – premonitions. I lately had one of you two being killed on my wedding day. Last night, I had one where I was standing right over there," I pointed to their window, "weeping about how I failed in protecting our kingdom."

Father and Mother stayed silent, but looked at me with wide eyes. "I'm scared," I added and began to cry. Mother wrapped her arm around me and Father leaned forward, elbows on his knees.

After a long moment of silence, Father asked, "Do you know who it is that kills us?"

My head shot up and I looked into his eyes. He believed me. Looking over to Mother, I could see that she did, too. Regaining eye contact with Father, I said, "No. He has been in several visions, though. David called him the Man of Night."

"David? He appears in your visions?" Mother asked.

"He used to, sometimes – before I met Harrison." I decided to leave out the fact that Harrison could read minds. That was his secret. "He would give me advice and comfort me when things were difficult, like when I was Frank's captive."

Father leaned back in his chair. "Interesting." Mother and I stared at him as he considered all the information I just gave him. "Does Phin know?"

"About my memories, yes, but not about my premonitions. Something stopped me from telling him."

"I think that's wise. Let's keep it that way for now. We will double security for the wedding day. For now, go on back to your room and make yourself presentable. King George XV and Queen Domonique will be arriving shortly after lunch today. Rehearsal will be this evening, followed by a small party with all the Nobles."

My jaw dropped. "That's it? We just continue as if nothing happened? What if King George is planning something?"

"It is best to go on as if nothing happened. Chances are, whoever is planning something will not be expecting security to be the size it will be tomorrow. Go on now, Rose. Adele should be to your room by now."

Nodding solemnly, I said something about being in agreement with him and left back to my room. Adele was, indeed, there and looked at me in horror. "You left your room like *that*?" Adele asked with a disgusted look on her face. "Did you even shower last night? Ew! That is the last time I let you –"

Whatever she was saying was lost over the sound of the shower starting and I smiled to myself. If I really did look as bad as she seemed to think, I was surprised my parents believed a word I had said.

After my shower, Adele and I had an argument over what I would wear. She wanted me to wear a full ball gown for the welcoming of King George XV and Queen Domonique, but I wasn't having it.

"No. Just – No, Adele. Did you see the giant monstrosity I am going to have to wear tomorrow?"

Adele gaped at me. "It is *not* a monstrosity! It is a *Braedon Tailor* dress! Do you even know what that means?"

"No. Should I?" I said, even though I did know what it meant. He was a highly sought after designer and I knew it, I just wanted to be disagreeable.

Wagging her finger at me, she said, "Fine! No ball gown, but you *will* wear this other Braedon Tailor dress in your closet. Really. The nerve –"

The words became mumbles under her breath as she swept her hands across the side of the long closet that held my dresses, finally stopping on an emerald green satin A-line dress. Holding it up, she raised her eyebrows to question my approval.

"Much better," I said, "but will I not be cold?"

Adele sniffed. "You will just have to hope they keep the heat on this evening. Besides, Prince Phineas is hot enough to keep you warm."

"Adele!"

"Well! He is!"

With more teasing and girly giggles, she continued to get me ready. It didn't take much longer to actually get me in the gown and do my hair and makeup. When she was done, I thanked her and went down to the library to see if there were any books on wedding ceremonies.

I tapped away at the Desk Computer and eventually discovered there was a book a couple stories up in the section of Arborian traditions. I climbed the stairs to the proper floor, then the ladder to get to the proper shelf.

"Rose?" Someone said my name below me and startled me. Though I tried to keep my balance, I fell, but was caught in someone's arms. I gasped as I had a flashback to a similar situation shortly before I went into my freeze.

"Déjà vu," I said and Peter chuckled. "Peter? What are you doing here? I thought you went home."

He set me down, then bent over to pick up the book I had dropped when I fell. "*Funerals, Weddings, and Other Arborian Ceremonies*. Wow, Rose. This sounds exciting."

Snatching the book back, I said, "Very funny, Peter. You know how my memory is." I marched over to the stairs and went back down to the first floor, Peter trailing behind me. "What do you need, Peter?"

"I'm here for the party tonight. Remember? All the Nobles will be here."

"Oh. That's right. I forgot you were in that group." I sighed and walked over to the window, hugging my book to my chest. "Something's not right, Peter. I feel like the problem is obvious and I'm not seeing it."

"Hmm," was all Peter said as he moved to stand next to me at the window.

"Do you trust Phin, Peter?"

"Phin? You mean Phineas? Your betrothed?" Peter teased.

"Yes. Him. Focus."

"Right." Peter shrugged and cleared his throat of the humor that had been sitting in it. "I suppose. He hasn't done anything to make me *not* trust him. He *was* among those of us who came to your rescue a few months ago."

"Yeah," I said almost under my breath.

Peter looked to me. "Do you not trust him?"

I began chewing on my thumb nail and shrugged.

"Rose! Have you told your parents?"

"No, but I *did* tell them about my premonitions."

Peter grabbed me by the arms and turned me so I was facing him. My eyes widened in shock and I continued to chew on my poor nail. "Have you had another one?"

"Two," I said, with my nail still in my mouth and extending two other fingers. Gently, he pulled my thumb from my mouth.

"What was it?" Peter asked.

As he released me, I told him about both visions. Calmly, he took it in, nodding at times that I knew he didn't really understand – because I didn't even understand myself. The whole time, he never broke eye contact with me, which I found more than a little unnerving.

"It's Frank," Peter said. "The Man of Night is Frank. That *has* to be it."

"That's what I think, too, but there's something off about Phin. Apparently, though, I'm the only one who feels that way."

The door slid open and we turned to look at the newcomer. It was Phin. I gave Peter a sidelong glance and hoped I didn't look as guilty as he did.

"Oh. Hello, Phineas," Peter said.

"Peter," Phin said in greeting. "I did not know you had arrived."

"He only just got here, as far as I know," I said with a shrug and walked over to Phin. When I got close enough, he grabbed my hand and pulled me into a possessive kiss. It was so unlike him, I did nothing to stop it. He stopped abruptly and said, "Lunch is ready. See you later, Peter."

Phineas gripped my hand hard and began pulling me to the Dining Hall. As we turned the corner and entered the Core, I finally yanked my hand free of his hand prison.

"What was that, Phin?" I demanded.

Glaring at me, he brought his face within inches of my own. "What were you doing in there with *him*?"

"Talking."

"About what?"

"My memories."

"Why were you talking with Peter about that? You have *me* for that now."

"Roots, Phin! There's no reason to be jealous." I took his hand gently and meekly looked down, hoping to calm the storm in his eyes. "He is the only friend I have left in this world and one of the only people who knows about my – problem."

Phin tilted my chin up so I was looking at his face and softened his expression. "I'm sorry for my reaction, Rose. It's unlike me to get jealous. It's just that – I know how close you two were at one point and when I found you alone in there – I became insecure. I know you don't love me yet –"

"I don't love Peter anymore, either. I can barely remember having loved him *before*." I placed a hand on his cheek. "There is nothing to be jealous of, Phin."

Phin took my hand and kissed my palm as he nodded. Taking my hand, he escorted me the rest of the way to the Dining Hall for lunch. My relaxed demeanor during our meal contradicted my true feelings

The way Phin had grabbed me and forced himself on me reminded me of when I had been in Frank's captivity. Always having been so kind to me in the past, I wondered how much of that was his true nature and how much of it was an act. I was also wondering if I was suffering from some serious PTSD and maybe should begin counseling again.

Peter joined Father, Mother, Phin, and I after a while and we all fell into awkward small talk. No one would make eye contact with anyone and Phin kept a hand on my leg the whole time as if laying a claim on me.

Finally, the Steward came in and announced the arrival of King George XV and Queen Domonique. I started to get up, but Phin held me down with his hand. "We will join you in a moment," he said to Father, Mother, and Peter.

Father nodded and escorted Mother from the room, but Peter waited for me to give him a nod before he turned and left.

"What is it now, Phin?" I asked, annoyed.

"Are you still mad at me?" he asked.

"I'm not mad," I responded honestly – I wasn't mad. I was scared.

"You haven't looked at me a single time since we came in here." I shrugged, but he tilted my chin again so I was looking at him. He looked full of regret. "Talk to me, Rose. After we welcome my brother and his wife, I don't know that we'll have much time alone together."

I swallowed the stone that had settled in my throat and argued with myself about whether or not I should continue being open with him. Deciding on the side of truth, I said, "You scared me in there, Phin. What you did – the way you forced yourself on me – that was the sort of thing Frank did when he held me prisoner. It makes me wonder how much you have actually been yourself with me. What will happen when you have the Crown and no longer need me to acquire it?"

Phin closed his eyes and covered his mouth with his hand as if in thought. Free from his hand, I looked back down at his other hand still holding my thigh. "Rose," he said and I looked back to him voluntarily. "I swear to you, I am not a jealous man. I am so sorry for what I did in the library. It will not happen again. Do you believe me?"

My mind screamed *No*, but my mouth said, "Yes." With a curt nod, Phin let go of my leg and took my hand.

"Now, let us go meet my brother and his wife," Phin said, leading me out the door. As we walked, I couldn't help but wonder how much like his brother Phin actually was.

Chapter 28

"Ah! Here they are," Father said as soon as he spotted Phin and me descending the Core. At his words, Phin picked up our speed and I let him, fixing a small smile on my face despite my anxiety. Seeing King George, I was reminded of the conversation we had ten years before and how angry he was over the King's Test.

Here's hoping he doesn't still hold a grudge.

Queen Domonique was a beautiful woman. She had the same chestnut brown hair as her brother, Leon, but her eyes were a deep blue rather than dark grey. While King George had a stoic expression, she had a bright smile. I liked her already.

When we reached the end of the stairs, Phin bowed and I curtseyed. Phin's brother and his wife mimicked our display of respect, but when we all rose, Queen Domonique threw her arms around me and whispered, "Welcome to the family *ma chérie*. I have heard so much about you and cannot wait to get to know you better!"

Surprised by her outburst of affection, I patted her gently on the back and whispered back, "I look forward to getting to know you, too." While we were embracing, Phin and his brother spoke in hushed tones. After she finally pulled away from me, King George took my hand and gave it a customary kiss.

"Crown Princess, it is a pleasure to finally meet you in person," King George said as he released my hand and straightened.

"And you, as well, King George," I responded. Though the words between us were friendly, the look in his eyes was icy.

Well, at least I know that he holds grudges. Yay new in-laws!

"It is a pity Father and Mother are not alive to see our great nations come together," King George said, then looking at his brother.

Phin nodded. "It certainly will be an historic moment for both our kingdoms."

I glanced over to Father, Mother, and Peter, all standing stoically still, witnessing our interactions. The only one who seemed genuinely pleased at the moment was Queen Domonique.

"It will be, indeed," Queen Domonique said. "Of course, I sort of had two horses in this race with Leon as well, but I am happy with this outcome. Both George and I are excited for what this union will bring our countries."

King George seemed to bristle at the mention of Queen Domonique's French brother and the reference to himself without his title.

"Queen Domonique, let us allow our men to visit with one another. Would you be interested in seeing my rose garden?" I asked.

"*Mais oui*! But I must insist you call me 'Domonique.' We are practically family!" she replied.

"Then you must call me 'Miriam.'" I responded and offered my arm to her. As she gracefully accepted, I said to Phin, "I will see you at dinner, love."

Phin's eyes widened at the endearment and he smiled. After kissing me on the cheek, he whispered into my ear, "Thank you for giving me another chance, Rose." I nodded with a demure smile and walked with Domonique to my rose garden without another word to anyone else.

When we entered the glass room, she brought a hand to her mouth and exclaimed, "It is even more beautiful than Leon said it was. All the colors of roses and they are in bloom in winter. How did you manage that?"

"I have amazing botanists who have figured out ways of making it happen," I replied, not knowing how I knew the information. "Quite honestly, I do not know much about gardening. I did design the maze, but the botanists put it together."

I brought her into the maze and led the way through it to the center. When Domonique saw the gazebo and sofa swing, she gasped. "This place is truly a treasure."

We sat on the sofa and began to swing it. Feeling brave, I said, "I do not think King George likes me very much."

Domonique waved her hand. "Oh. Never mind him. The Britainnians in general tend to be pretty bland emotionally. He will get used to you."

I laughed at her assessment of the Britainnians, then said, "How is it that you and King George got together?"

"It was arranged shortly after you went into your freeze. At first, I was unhappy with the arrangement. George is well-known for his short temper and lack of compassion. Over time, though, I have come to love him and I would like to think he loves me."

"You would like to think? He does not tell you?"

"I do not know that he knows how. But I have done everything I should have. Our son is at home – he is five. That was my job."

"Do you not hate it sometimes, Domonique? That we did not get to choose our husbands?"

She hesitated before answering. "Sometimes, yes. But you need not worry about Phineas. He is much different than his brother."

I nodded and leaned my head against the rope of the swing. "He has already told me he loves me."

Domonique's eyes widened in her surprise. "Really? That was fast. Though, look at you. Most likely the most beautiful woman in the world."

I laughed. "Are you kidding? Have you looked in a mirror?"

For the next hour or so, we sat and chatted about life and flowers. I liked Domonique and was glad she would soon be my sister-in-law, even if she did live far away from Arboria.

In the middle of a childish giggle fit, King George and Phin appeared in the archway. Phin smiled and King George looked as though he was fighting one.

Perhaps this won't be so bad after all. Domonique is lovely and she trusts Phin. I must just be paranoid.

"There you are," said King George, and Domonique waved at him with her delicate fingers.

"I told you they would still be here. This is Miriam's favorite place. She could spend hours here," Phin said with amusement spread all over his face.

"Understandable. Am I to understand you designed this room?" King George asked with a tinge of admiration in his voice.

I nodded and stood. Domonique did as well and we both stretched involuntarily at the same time in the same way, which sent us into another fit of giggles.

Rolling his eyes, King George said, "Come along Domonique. It is time to get ready for our dinner in an hour."

"An hour?!" She and I both exclaimed in horror simultaneously and this time, the men both chuckled. Domonique rushed over to King George.

"George! Why did you not come for me sooner? An hour is not much time. How am I supposed to –" Domonique continued in a string of French that I couldn't follow.

King George lightly placed his finger on her lips to silence the tirade of foreign concern pouring out. "You are already beautiful, love. It will not take long to get ready, I am sure." He bent down and kissed her delicately. "Alright, then. We will see you both in an hour."

Phin waved them off and I walked over to him as they left. Setting aside the concerns I had earlier, I melted into him and allowed him to hold me for the moment. "Ah – this is – unexpected. Is everything alright, Rose?"

I nodded into his chest. "Things are wonderful, Phin." I looked up to him. "I think things will be just fine."

Chapter 29

The Nobles joined us in the Dining Hall for dinner to begin the evening. Everyone was excited to meet King George and Queen Domonique; we did not receive foreign Royalty very often. Phin and I sat quietly next to each other. Because I was nervous, my plate went fairly untouched.

Phin kept his left hand on my leg throughout dinner, but he wasn't gripping me possessively like he had been earlier in the day. Since my afternoon with Domonique, I was feeling pretty positive about the future. Dismissing my fears of Phin as paranoia from the traumatic experience of being Frank's captive, I decided to accept my future with open arms.

After dinner, we went to the Main Ballroom and did a quick run-through of the wedding. The actual event would take place at the church in the center of Petrichoria, but with the increase in security, we thought it best to keep as much as possible within the walls of Evergreen Palace.

Standing across from Phin with the Pastor and our families was a bit surreal and it made my head spin as I considered what it all meant for me. Soon, I would be expected to produce an heir to the Crown of Arboria, which meant Phin and I would –

It's not like I don't know how. David and I did it. But this is a whole new body and a whole new life.

I buried the thoughts of the wedding night six feet under into my brain and tried to focus on the moment. Phin was giving me a quizzical look as if he could tell my mind had wandered and I blushed furiously, hoping he couldn't figure out what I had been thinking about. The smirk he gave me after seeing me blush told me my hope was in vain.

" – And this is the part where I declare you man and wife and Prince Phineas will kiss his bride," the Pastor was saying.

Phin took me in his arms and kissed me passionately and everyone present cheered and whistled. My knees went weak beneath me and when Phin pulled away, he had to help me stand upright. We practiced our departure, then reentered the room for the rehearsal party.

However, it didn't go that simply for me. When we came back into the Main Ballroom, everything went black and I fell to the ground. I heard the rush of footsteps, and muffled voices. My eyes were open, but I wasn't seeing the ballroom or anyone present anymore.

Flashes of my past sped before me and my heart raced as everything rushed back into my mind. As the memories poured in like a flood, I screamed in pain.

Wearing a sparkly pink leotard, my seven-year-old self completes an acrobatic dance to a contemporary pop song on a balance beam in the Main Ballroom.

Ms. Elise says, "Very good, Princess Miriam. You are still stumbling a bit on your landings, so practice a couple times on your own before your recital tomorrow night.

I smile broadly and nod.

Vaguely, I felt myself lifted into someone's arms and the wind of being carried through a hall and up the Core.

I am fourteen and scrambling up a tree to get to a treehouse. Shortly after I make it, a boy slightly older than me throws his legs up and hauls himself up. Stephan. Yes. That's who it is.

"I win!" I shout in victory with my arms in the air.

"You always do, Rose," Stephan says.

Tilting my head like a curious cat, I say, "You don't let me win, do you?"

Stephan drops to the floor and stretches out all the way lengthwise with a sigh. "If I did, I wouldn't tell you."

I plop down next to him and cross my legs. Taking a string of flowers from the pocket of my vest, I begin stringing them into a crown.

"Tell me again, Stephan. Tell me about when we met," I beg as I weave the flowers.

Stephan sighs and rubs a long hand down his face. "Rose, I've told you that story a million times. What matters is that we're friends now, right?"

As I place my crude crown on his head, he turns and looks at me seriously. I lay next to him and snuggle in as he pets my hair. "No. We're not friends," I say.

"What?" he stops with my hair and looks down to me, making him appear chinless.

"You are my brother and I am your sister," I say with a smile.

My breathing was shallow as memories from my childhood and teenage years came in. Somewhere in the back of my mind, I knew Doctor Quincy had arrived and was examining me.

"Doctor Bartholomew, is this really necessary?" I ask my tutor.

"Of course it is, Miriam. Again. Tell me about the United States and what it was." He demands.

Lesson after lesson with Doctor Bartholomew came back to me and I suddenly knew all the traditions and histories I knew before.

"It's just the way it has always been, Rose. I really don't know what the big deal is anyway. It's not like you're being asked to fall in love with seven men. This evening is a demonstration that you are worth more than the Crown. A kiss is personal and can help bring things into perspective for the participants. At least you only have seven; I had twelve at the beginning of my Queen's Test. A set of triplets, even!" Father says.

I coo, "Oh. Poor boy. Father, kisses don't mean as much to a man as they do to a woman. For a woman, she gives love with a kiss. A man just takes possession."

"That is not fair, Rose. And it is not true. I know you don't like some of the men participating, but give them a chance. I'll bet there is more to every man than he shows the public."

Memories of how I felt about the tradition of the King's Test come forth. Not surprising, it wasn't much different than how I felt now.

One of the participants lays on his death bed, suffering hallucinations from the mutated Daze. Linc.

Linc swallows hard. His lips are dry. I lean over him and press my glossed lips softly on his parched ones. A kiss goodbye for him. He lets out a sigh of relief.

"I'm so sorry, Rose," Linc says.

"Whatever for?" I ask.

"For the tulips," he says, confirming my thought that he is delirious.

I smile at him. "It's alright. I think tulips are beautiful, especially in the spring."

He is still looking me in the eyes. "But you love the roses, my sweet Rose of Petrichoria."

I smile at him and dam up the tears trying to escape my eyes. "Oh, but don't you know? Tulips are my second favorite. What do you say? When you get out of here, should we plant some in my garden?"

"I would love that. Is that a part of the Test?"

"No. This will be something special for us." I make a mental note to plant some tulips in my garden to remember these men who could have been my husband.

"Must plant tulips," I muttered in delirium.

"Alright, Rose," someone male responded to me and dabbed my forehead with a cool cloth.

I'm talking with Peter on the holocomm in a sterile room and his eyes are full of tears. As I open my mouth to speak, the door to the quarantine room slides open and Doctor Mage pushes in a cryogenic chamber.

"I thought I had an hour," I say. Peter's brow furrows and more tears fall down his face.

"I did not realize there was anyone here. I am getting it set up. It should not take long. I am pretty much ready when you are."

I swallow and turn my attention back to Peter while the doctors set everything up.

"Peter, I'm scared," I say.

"I know. Me, too," Peter replies.

I chuckle breathily. "That's not very comforting."

"Neither are you," he says and laughs dryly at his own joke. "Ella's right, you know."

"What? That she shouldn't be Queen? I know she hasn't had the training, but –"

"Don't do that," Peter pleads.

"What?"

"Make light of this. There is nothing light about this."

"I know. I just hate seeing you so sad."

"I wish I could kiss you one more time. I wish I had said and done a thousand other things when I saw you this morning. Had I known this would happen, I would have done things differently."

"True tragedy is never expected, my love. That's why we have to live every moment as if tragedy is right around the corner. I love you."

"I love you, too."

"Princess," Doctor Mage says and waits for me to look at him. "I am ready when you are."

"Alright, Doctor." I look back at Peter. "I'm going to go to sleep now, Peter. I'll see you when I wake up."

"I love you."

"I love you, too."

"I'll be here." He disconnects.

Slowly, my real vision began to reform in my eyes. I figured not much time had passed because Phin was leaning over me with a worried expression on his face. Blinking some tears in my eyes, I said, "How long?"

Phin breathed a sigh of relief and kissed me soundly. "Not long. Only about a half hour. People are still downstairs. They were told you fainted from exhaustion and stress and would be back down soon."

I chuckled. My voice hurt from screaming and my brain hurt from the memory dump. "I remembered."

"What?"

I looked into Phin's eyes and smiled. "I remembered everything."

Chapter 30

"You remembered everything?" Phin repeated what I had just said.

"Yes. My childhood. My lessons with Doctor Bartholomew. The events that took place before my freeze. Everything," I said with a giant smile plastered on my face, trying to sit up. The room became fuzzy and Phin reached over to help me.

"That's fantastic, Rose!" Phin said, returning my smile with his own.

"Let's get back to the party," I said, but Phin laughed and kept me down.

"You can barely sit up straight. Are you sure you want to go down?" Phin asked me.

"You can be my crutch."

"What if someone else wants to dance with you?"

I shrugged. "Then *they* will be my crutch. They all know I passed out – they'll understand."

Phin laughed and shook his head. "Alright, but we won't stay for long. We have a long day tomorrow and – a long night, too." He waggled his eyebrows at me and I rolled my eyes at him.

"Fine, fine. Just get me out of bed."

With a chuckle, Phin laced his arm under mine and lifted me from the bed. As I straightened out, I wrapped my arm around his waist and he shuffled around so our movements were less awkward.

On our way down the Core, I asked, "Did you carry me all the way up to my room from the second floor?"

"Mmm hmm."

"Wow."

"What? You would have done the same."

"I would have *wanted* to do the same," I joked and Phin snorted. "Seriously, though. Thank you, Phin. Today has been very enlightening."

"You're welcome, love. How do you mean, 'enlightening?'"

"I feel like I have gotten to know you more in the last twenty-four hours than I have in the past several months."

"To be fair, two of those months, you were gone and one of them, you were recovering."

"That's a nice way of saying I was the prisoner of a lunatic and needed time to recuperate from starving myself in a hunger strike."

"Yes, it is." Phin smiled again.

When we stepped into the Main Ballroom, everyone applauded. Phin held up his free hand to quiet the crowd, then said, "My bride was feeling a bit flustered with our upcoming nuptials, but is doing much better now. We will not be staying for long, but she insisted on making sure everyone knew she is feeling much better and is looking forward to tomorrow's events."

Everyone applauded again and I saw Peter rush forward. Several feet away from me, he stopped and glanced to Phin as if asking for permission to approach. I felt Phin nod once and Peter came the rest of the way, bowing politely when he got to us.

"May I please have this dance, Crown Princess?" Peter asked. I could tell he was trying to make up for what had happened earlier in the library with the formality the Britannians seemed to love.

I looked to Phin, who nodded with a smile and I offered my hand to Peter. The waltz began and Peter held me close so I could keep my balance. "Are you alright, Rose?" he asked so only I could hear.

How can I tell him without giving away the problem I have had for so long?

"I feel better than I have since before going into my freeze," I said.

Peter furrowed his brow. "What?"

I smiled. "Do you remember the time you and Stephan competed to see who could skip rocks the furthest?"

Peter's eyes widened, then smiled bigger than he had when the Council voted 'aye' on our engagement ten years before. "You won."

I fought pulling my friend into a fierce embrace – it would have been horribly inappropriate. At the end of the dance, Father swooped me up into his arms for another dance. I shared the news with him by reminiscing about a book he used to read to me every night before bed and he said he would "share the memory with Mother later on."

After several more dances, King George approached for a dance. I looked to Domonique, who gestured with her hand for me to go ahead. "I apologize, Your Majesty, but I am still needing some assistance with staying up. You will need to hold me close."

King George obliged and said, "Please, call me George. You are practically my sister now. Have you been starting all your dances with that phrase?"

I chuckled. "Yes – except the 'Your Majesty' was specific to you. You may call me Miriam."

George gave me a real smile for the first time all day; for the first time *ever*, in fact. "A lot has happened over the last ten years, Miriam."

"So I have noticed. Domonique is a lovely woman. You are blessed to have her."

"I suppose I have you to thank for our marriage." George laughed at his own joke.

Smiling, I said, "Not just me, but the Arborian Council, as well."

After a pause, George said, "I *am* sorry for my deplorable attitude all those years ago."

I shrugged it off. "It was ten years ago, George. I am not one to hold a grudge."

"I understand, though, that it does not feel like ten years to you. I would hate for my arrogant attitude of my youth to influence your impression of me now."

252

"All is forgiven, brother," I said as the song ended. Phin came up then and took my hand gently in his.

"One more dance, then it is back to bed for you, Rose," he said, enfolding me into his strong arms for a slow song. George bowed and rejoined Domonique, bringing her onto the dancefloor.

"Yes, Father," I teased.

Phin glared at my taunt. Ever so quietly, he whispered in my ear, "I'm not into that, Rose."

I choked on my laughter, which made Phin laugh as well. The Nobles around us looked at us strangely and I was sure I turned a bright shade of red. "How did I get so lucky to have you as my bride?"

Tilting my head, I said, "Luck had nothing to do with it. The only thing you're *lucky* for is that the woman you won is not only beautiful, but quirky and intelligent."

Phin snorted. "And so humble, too." We danced with only the sound of the string instruments for a moment. "You know – I don't think you that way, right Rose?"

"What way is that?"

"A prize. You said I 'won' you. I don't think of you as a prize I have won."

Rolling my sore shoulders, I said, "I don't mean anything personal by it, Phin. But you must admit, that is exactly what has happened. You *won* me and the Crown that comes with me." I looked down at Phin's chest, which was only a couple inches from my face, and he rested his cheek on my head. "I suppose that could explain part of my paranoia earlier today in the library. And I suppose that is one of the biggest differences between you and Frank."

I brought my face back to look at him and he only turned his head, so it brought our faces close together. "When Frank told me he didn't view me as a prize to be won, he demonstrated the complete opposite with everything he did. I was a conquest for him and his actions declared me as such." The song ended, but we stayed like that on the edge of the dancefloor.

"When you tell me I am not a prize to you, I believe you mean it. You have been kind and endearing to me – you have cherished me even before we are married and that bodes well for our future together."

Phin pressed his lips softly against mine and said, "Let's get you back to your room. Time to rest up for tomorrow." Ever so gently, Phin took my arm in his. We bid our guests farewell and he helped me up the Core to my room.

Handing me over to Adele for the night, he whispered good night, then left to his own room. After Adele helped me shower and get ready for bed, she tucked me into my blankets. "Thank you, Adele," I mumbled as I drifted to sleep.

"You are very welcome, dear friend," she said.

Chapter 31

"Hello, Miriam."

I turn around in the room of white to see a face I didn't expect to ever see again.

"David," I breathe. "What are you doing here?"

"Well, seems like you need me again."

I nod. "Yes. Harrison left. Not that he or I had much choice in the matter."

"He misses you."

"And I him."

"Have you been on the lookout for the Man of Night?"

"You know better than anyone I have been trying to figure out who he is. I keep coming back to Frank, but it seems so obvious. If it is Frank, why haven't I just seen him? In fact, why is the Man of Night be a mystery at all? Where are these premonitions even coming from? I cannot figure out a scientific answer to any of my questions."

"Perhaps the answer isn't scientific."

"What? Like God?"

David says nothing, but smiles.

"God? Seriously?"

David shrugs. "Seems as good an answer as any. Remember, I am your subconscious. I can only give you answers you think of all on your own. Talking to me is essentially talking to yourself."

"But – God? It seems like if He was going to give me premonitions, they would be a little clearer."

"Have you read Revelation?"

"Point taken." I sigh. "Why me?"

"I think every great man and woman in history asked themselves that question more than once in their lifetimes."

"You think I am going to be great?"

"Of course. I'm you. And, as Phin said earlier, you are very *humble."*

"Very funny, David."

David takes my hand and we stand still for a moment. Just him and me against my real life and the insanity that surrounds it.

"Maybe the obvious answer is *the answer this time," David says.*

"What?"

"Frank. Maybe he is *the Man of Night."*

"I don't know how he could possibly infiltrate the palace or chapel tomorrow. We have more security than the President on Inauguration Day stationed everywhere."

"Maybe he has an inside man?"

I shrug. "That's possible, though Father has been quite thorough in his hiring since Frank's betrayal."

"Maybe it isn't someone who has been hired."

"Like one of the Nobles or Delegates? How do you think he could get to them?"

"Promises of more wealth? More power? Greed is an animal with insatiable hunger. All he would need to do is find the right person to feed."

I move to sit and a white bench appears beneath me. "This is too much. Why can't I just get married to my Brit and have a normal life?"

David sits next to me, still holding my hand. "You are going to be Queen someday, Miriam. 'Normal' has never really been a part of your future."

"Do you like him? Phin?"

"Do you?"

"I hate when you do that. I hated when you did it when you were living and I hate it when you do that here."

"What?"

"Answer a question with a question. It's like you're some mage from a fantasy novel."

David laughs his hearty laugh, and I can't help but end my pout and smile. After a sigh, he says, "I do like him. Phin. I don't completely trust him, but I like him."

"Me, too. I suppose as long as he has the best interest of Arboria and me at heart, that's all that matters."

"Loyalty matters, too."

"Is that where you think he's lacking? Loyalty?"

"He doesn't say much about his family, does he?"

I think about all our conversations over the last few days. "I suppose not, but none of the men spoke of their families much."

"Hmm."

"Hmm, indeed."

David brushes my hand with his thumb. "I am glad you got your memory back, Miriam."

"Me, too. I'm even happier that I was able to maintain the memories of my false life, too. I was afraid that when my real memories returned, they would push the others out."

"What color are my eyes?"

"What? They're brown, of course." I look into his eyes and find them blue. "Oh. Blue. Kona-blue. That's right."

"What are the names of our children?"

I think so hard, my brain starts to hurt. "What is happening? I can picture them, but I can't remember their names. Why can't I remember our children, David?"

"I don't know. Maybe you were right about your real life memories."

"I don't want to forget you."

"I'm not important."

"Of course you're important. We were married for – for – gah! I can't remember how long we were married!"

David places his hands on my shoulders. "Breathe, Miriam. It's alright. I'm here as long as you need me, remember?"

"How is it that I can remember you and who you are, but specific memories seem to be lost?"

"Because I'm here as long as you need me."

"I need you."

"I know. That's why I'm still here. I'm kind of feeling like a broken record, Miriam."

I chuckle. "Don't leave me, David. I have a feeling something horrible is around the corner. I told Father and Mother about my vision, but I am afraid that even with that, there is no stopping something horrid from happening."

"I think you're right. Your biggest trial is coming up. You've been through so much already, but I know something much harder will happen."

"Tomorrow?"

David nods. "I think it's likely."

"Do you think I should contact Harrison? Make sure he's keeping an eye on things?"

259

"I am," I turn away from David and see Harrison sitting on my other side.

"Harrison," I whisper and David disappears.

"What are you doing here? I thought we agreed to not see each other like this anymore." I say, like the hypocrite I am. Most likely, I was the one who brought him here.

"We did. We're not seeing each other. Just checking in."

"How much of that conversation did you hear?"

"Honestly?"

I nod.

"All of it."

"Not even any privacy in my dreams."

"You and I both know this isn't just a dream."

"Do you agree with David? That these – gifts – are from God?"

"It's possible. I haven't found any scientific answer for it either."

"When my memories returned, I remembered that I was having these visions even before my freeze. The doctor responsible for the mutated Daze knew about it and tested me frequently for any abnormalities and never found anything in any scan or test. Maybe it is God."

"Maybe." Harrison pauses. "I'm keeping my eyes open, Rose. If anything even seems a little off tomorrow, I will begin meeting with my sister, the Queen, as soon as possible."

I chortle. "I don't know what you can do from down in Southland. My latest vision shows my parents being killed tomorrow by the Man of Night. Whatever you can do will be too late for that if it happens."

"Perhaps your increase in security will hamper the Man of Night's plans."

"Perhaps."

The desire to fall into Harrison's arms is overwhelming, but I refuse to allow myself to do it. I am engaged to Phin.

"Has he been kind to you?" Harrison asks.

I smile sadly, knowing he can read my conflicting emotions. "Of course. You can read my thoughts," I realize aloud. "We had an – incident – this morning when Peter arrived, but aside from that, he has been very kind and loving. He has told me numerous times he loves me and has been very patient with me. He knows how I feel about you. I wish it was you."

"I know. I wish it was me, too."

"What are you going to do? Will your sister make an arrangement for you?"

"Uh – no. I am in no rush to get over you and move on. If I wait too long, she will probably prod me to some woman of her choice, but she will never force me to marry anyone. Just as our parents never made her choose anyone. She's still single, you know."

"I didn't know, but I am glad for both of you. When I am Queen, I am placing the choice of spouse for my heir into his or her hands. I will not have them go through this pain."

"You're a good woman, Rose."

"If I was such a good woman, I would not be spending the night before my wedding with a man who isn't my groom."

"Men you mean. I'm not the only man invading your thoughts tonight."

I laugh. "David doesn't count. He is essentially me."

Harrison sobers. "I'm sorry you're losing them."

I know he means my family from my false life. "Me, too. Hopefully, I've told enough people that they can help me remember them. Really, all I can remember is the time period, David, and the fact that we had children – a boy and a girl."

"Tom and Harmony."

"That's right. You remembered?"

"I remember everything about you, Rose. I don't think I'll ever forget."

We look into each other's eyes for a few painful moments before I break our connection and look at my fiddling fingers. "You should probably be going, Harrison. Thank you, though, for watching out for me."

Harrison takes my hand and kisses it. "I will always be watching out for you, Rose." He disappears.

I sit alone on my bench in my white space and wonder just how alone I am in the world now that I have gained the memories of my life and lost the ones I shouldn't have had to begin with.

Chapter 32

"Today is the day!" Adele bounced in singing something I knew she had made up, but I was so groggy from the long dream, I didn't catch the words. My dress stood over by one of the trees in the room on a mannequin and I eyed it. Having gotten my memory back, I realized that the reason the rotting thing was so heavy was because it was laced with armor. I briefly wondered if Phin's tux was as well or if Braedon Tailor only felt the need to make sure the Crown Princess was protected.

Shoving the pillow over my head, I mumbled, "Let me sleep a little longer. Just get me to the church on time."

Suddenly, the blankets and pillows were ripped off by Adele and gooseflesh spread all over my body. "Rotting roots! Why is it so cold?"

"It is December, Miriam. That is why."

Giving her a dirty look, I said, "You turn the heat off in here before waking me up in the morning, do you not?"

Smirking with a knowing grin, she said, "I have no idea what you are talking about. Let me get you a nice warm shower going." Adele turned to go into the bathroom.

"That is just evil!" I shouted after her and she laughed maniacally.

Flipping over to my back, I stared at the ceiling.

I am getting married today. I am marrying Prince Phineas of Britainnia today.

I covered my face with my hands.

I wish I could remember my wedding night with David – then maybe I wouldn't be feeling so nervous.

Before I could lament the loss of my false life, Adele rushed in and said, "My Fair Lady, right?"

Uncovering my face, I looked at her quizzically. "What?"

"You said 'Just get me to the church on time.' You were referencing that *really really really* old musical that you referred me to, right?"

I thought about it, realizing I had, indeed, subconsciously referenced the film. "Huh. Yeah. Good job, Adele."

I stood and stretched and Adele gently shoved me to the bathroom. "Come along, Crown Princess. I let you sleep in because of your little incident last night, but we need to get moving now."

"What time is it?" I asked as I pulled off my nightgown and stepped into the shower. I immediately began scrubbing down with my rose-scented soaps.

"10:00"

"What?! You realize the wedding is at 1:00, right?"

"Yes. That is why we must hurry."

"I mean. Do not get me wrong. I love sleep, Adele, but, blossoms. That hardly gives me time to calm my nerves."

I stepped out of the shower and a knocking came at the door. Adele tossed me my towel and ran to answer it. After wrapping my hair in a towel, I peeked out of the bathroom to make sure the door had been closed. On my little table was a vase of roses and a tea tray. Adele was holding a note and read it melodramatically out loud.

"Dearest Rose,

I know you must be having some nerves this morning. As I was having my own tea to calm myself, I thought of you and decided to have some authentic Britainnian tea sent to you. I will see you at 1:00, love.

With All My Heart,

Phin"

Snatching the note from Adele, I blushed furiously. "Notes are *private* Adele," I chastised softly with a tint of embarrassment and she giggled.

"Oh. He sent two cups!"

"I suppose I should offer you the other cup," I said in mock defeat. "Pour the tea while I stick my hair in the dryer."

A while later, we were sipping tea as she meticulously wrapped rubies and diamonds into an intricate updo with lots of tiny braids. She did my face simply with pinks and shimmery whites and before I knew it, it was 12:15 and I was getting into my gigantic dress.

I looked at myself in the mirror, finally believing the beauty standing there was me. No longer feeling like I was looking at a stranger, I smiled and put my long gloves on. Adele placed my

Crown Princess tiara strategically on my head and hugged me before I opened the door.

When I stepped out, Father and Mother stood completely still. Mother brought a handkerchief to her eyes and dabbed, and Father's eyes twinkled with unshed tears. "Don't you dare start crying," I said to them and they rushed me with a tight embrace.

"I am so glad you have your memory back for today. You know how long you and I have dreamed of this day," Mother said to me. I was glad for it, too. The dress, I remembered, was exactly what she and I had drawn up with Braedon Tailor ten years earlier, with a few updates from Adele, and it was more beautiful than either of us imagined it would be.

Father kissed my forehead, then offered his arm, which I gratefully accepted. "I keep telling myself not to cry, but I'm not sure I can make it through the whole ceremony."

Mother took Father's other arm and the three of us descended the Core. On the bottom floor, Evergreen Palace's staff and Guards that were not attending at the chapel circled around and applauded when we reached them. As we walked past, I heard murmurs of well-wishing and nodded in acceptance of them.

Louis was in his dress uniform and opened the front doors for us and my new day Guard, whose name I had yet to obtain, opened the hover's doors. The three of us piled in and tried desperately not to cry on our way over to the chapel. Father and I were successful. Mother? Not so much.

Closing my eyes, I tried to picture my wedding day with David, but couldn't. It was probably all for the best, anyway. I was getting ready to begin a new life again, with Phin. There really was no purpose in trying to compare the two of them when they were probably very different men.

The doors to the church were old and opened out rather than slid open. Just on the other side was the sanctuary where we would marry, so Father, Mother, and I waited patiently for the musical cue to go in.

High General Miller bowed to us when he opened the doors. It made me feel safe to know that the highest ranking official was in charge of security. Nothing was going to interrupt this special day.

The wedding, though extravagant and commed to the whole world, had a limited number of people present. I was disappointed to see none of the Delegates decided to come, but all the Nobles were there.

Phin was handsome as ever, standing at the altar of the church in his tailored tuxedo and his brother and sister-in-law stood behind him in place of his parents. I took my place across from him, Father and Mother moving to stand behind me.

Leaning toward me, Phin whispered with a nervous smile, "Are you ready, Rose?"

Feeling heat rise to my cheeks, I whispered in return, "I have never felt more ready."

Chapter 33

The moment Phin lurched forward and gripped me by my waist, I knew something was off. When he pulled me to him, I frowned in confusion. When he dropped us to the floor and covered me, I screamed.

Truth be told, I was also screaming over the loud, high-pitched sounds coming from the back of the room. That area was being blocked from my view by Phin's body, but I heard two giant thuds behind me and two behind the spot Phin had been standing. The screeching sounds I had been hearing stopped. Sounds of scurrying feet told me the Nobles were running out of the room and I wondered how they were getting past whatever was going on.

"Phin, what is going on?" I whispered in the now silent room and I heard a singular slow clap begin near the back of the room.

"I'm sorry, Rose. This is for the best," Phin said as he stood up and walked out of the room – past Frank, Frank's father, and a line of Frank's men without a glance.

"Phin!" I shouted, but he kept moving. I glanced over to where he had been standing and saw George and Domonique lying dead. "Traitor!" I yelled and he stopped. Realization hit me then and I turned my head around, seeing Father and Mother dead behind me.

"No!" I shrieked, managed to pull roll off the steps of the altar to shove myself up, and took off after Phin. As I got closer to him, I could hear High General Miller and the men's light guns buzzing with the tell-tale sign they had just been fired – on the Nobles, my parents, and Phin's brother and sister-in-law.

"I trusted you! I almost *loved* you!" I exclaimed with tears streaming down my face. Before I reached him, High General Miller grabbed my wrist and spun me around. In my peripheral vision, I saw Phin take off in a run, probably too much of a coward to face me, and Frank laughed. With my free hand, I surprised the High General by taking his gun from his hand and aiming at him. The men all raised their guns at me, but Frank signaled for them to lower them.

Quickly, High General Miller released me and Frank stopped laughing. Both men held their hands out in front of them. "Now, Crown Princess. No one wants to hurt you," High General Miller said, though his slow hand reaching behind him said otherwise to me.

"High General Miller. You are a traitor to this kingdom. I hereby sentence you to death." It was a mouthful, but I said it fast and shot him with the same weapon he had more-than-likely just used on my parents and the rulers of Britainnia. As High General Miller fell to his knees, Frank launched himself at me and got me to the floor again. Wrestling the gun from my hands, he threw it across the room. "Let me go!" I screamed at him, trying to scratch him with my well-manicured claws. Somehow, he managed to lay himself over me and trap me beneath him, but I still struggled to get away.

"Bring him in!" Frank shouted, then he leaned into my ear and whispered. "Thank you for killing my father. That would have been a hard thing for me to do personally." His whisper of gratitude shocked me into stillness and I gaped at him.

"Unhand me!" Peter shouted as he was dragged in by a couple Guards that I now recognized from my time in captivity on the island. They threw him to his knees next to me and pointed the light gun at his head. "Peter," I whispered as I turned my head to the side.

"That's right," Frank said, only a couple inches from my ear. Holding both wrists with one hand above my head, he turned my face back to him. "There's no running. Let's be real, there's no getting up in this dress by yourself now that you're laying down on a flat floor. If you do not begin cooperating, I will have Peter shot dead."

"No! You can't marry him, Rose!" Peter shouted and was slapped upside the head for it.

I swallowed hard. "He's right," I croaked. "I won't surrender this kingdom to you for one person."

Though I was still facing Frank, I saw Peter's head droop at my statement. I had a feeling that even if I *did* cooperate, he would kill Peter anyway.

Frank sighed and narrowed his eyes at me. "Very well." He nodded and the soldier moved to shoot him in the head.

Time froze as my sight blurred into a vision.

White space surrounds me now and I am standing in a simple green halter dress. Frantically, I look around, trying to figure out what is going on, until I finally see him. Peter.

Running to his arms, I weep and allow him to coo at me and stroke my hair. "I'm sorry, Peter! There is nothing I can do!"

"You're doing this somehow," Peter says. "What is this?"

"I don't know. My mind's desperation for me to say goodbye. This might not even be real. You might not even be here. I have only ever really seen Harrison in my head."

"Harrison?"

I shrug. "He can read minds."

"Of course, he can. How could I even think to compete with a man who could see your thoughts?"

"I don't want to talk about that. I'm sorry I doubted you. I'm sorry that I won't be able to ask your forgiveness for real."

"There is nothing to forgive, but I think I really am here."

"Then tell me something you would know that I wouldn't. I will find evidence of it somehow and know I was really able to say goodbye to you."

"There is only one thing I can think of and I am not sure you will be able to find evidence of it. Perhaps if you talk with Doctor Quincy –"

"Just tell me. I don't know how long this vision will last."

"It's a confession, I'm afraid. But I suppose there is nothing left to lose." Peter sighs. "It was me. I was the man who opened your freezing chamber."

I pull back and look in his moistened chocolate brown eyes. "What?"

"I had it open too long. Doctor Quincy warned me if it was open for longer than a minute, there could be unintended consequences, but I couldn't not kiss you one last time."

"Why? Why would you open it, knowing there were risks?"

"I had decided to marry Ella and guilt had become a close enemy. He followed me everywhere I went and in everything I did. I had to see you, to beg your forgiveness, not knowing if you could even hear me. I suppose now I know you couldn't. Please forgive my selfishness, Rose. Before I die, I must know you forgive me."

"I forgive you, Peter."

In the next moment, my sight returned and I saw the soldier shoot Peter in the head without ceremony. His body immediately went slack and the soldier kicked him in the back, sending him face first into the floor.

"No!" I screamed in Frank's face and began struggling again, crying anew.

"It's too bad he didn't just die when he was supposed to with the Duchess Elleouise and their little brat," he said through clenched teeth as he tried to get me still again.

"I knew it! I knew you killed them! I'll never cooperate! You will never rule Arboria!"

"Here's my second offer," Frank said with maddening calm after subduing me again. "I have bombs planted in the capitals of each province. If you don't marry me right now, I will signal to have them go off. Thousands will die. You know I won't hesitate. I am *done* playing nice, Miriam."

"You're lying!" I yelled.

"Do you really want to bet on that?"

I sniffed and stilled, feeling the muscles in his legs relax a little. Both of us were breathing heavily after our fight. "What if the Pastor refuses?" I asked, hoping the man of God would at least be faithful to me.

Frank chuckled. "Are you kidding? This is the same Pastor who baptized me three years ago. He will *gladly* perform the ceremony."

Tilting my head back, I looked upside down to the Pastor who smiled at me and waited peacefully among the dead to marry Frank and me. "You killed them," I wheezed, closing my eyes.

"I will kill *more* if you won't do this."

Gazing back into his cruel eyes, I said, "I will never love you."

"At the moment, I don't really care. I'll worry about that later."

I felt my lower lip tremble as I considered my options. Technically, Frank would not be King until he was coronated. The only thing the wedding would accomplish would make him my husband.

Pressing my lips tightly together, I nodded slowly and a cry squeaked out of my throat. Smiling triumphantly, Frank gently maneuvered himself off me and offered me his hand to help me up. Begrudgingly, I accepted – he was right – there was no way to get to standing on my own in the gown.

Stepping over the dead bodies of High General Miller and Peter, he escorted me back to the front of the sanctuary. It sickened me that Frank could turn on his regality in the middle of such death and destruction. As if to rub it in, Frank stationed me in front of my dead parents and his guards replaced George and Domonique with his dead father.

Everything that happened had been commed all over the world. I silently prayed for the safety of Phin's nephew and for the safety of my people.

Turning to the Pastor, I said, "God will judge you for your treachery. When I get my kingdom back, I will send you to Him."

Chapter 34

After a deep swallow of saliva, and just a moment of hesitation, the Pastor wasted no further time with the ceremony. He skipped over the floral language of the traditional Arborian wedding. Essentially, he only had us exchange rings – I was disgusted when Frank simply bent over and removed his father's wedding band for himself. Of course, he had a band for me in his pocket.

After the ceremony, Frank and I rode back to Evergreen Palace in my hover. There was rioting in the streets and anyone who tried to help me was shot. Though I had pled for everyone to stay in their homes, some chose to fight. I couldn't blame them; I only hoped they could figure out a way to organize underground and help retake the kingdom.

On the way over, Frank played his favorite game of pinning me against the wall – or door, in this case. Although I was able to keep my lips from his, he kissed my neck and whispered about how excited he was for the coming night because I was finally *his*.

Gripping my arm, he pulled me up the stairs of the Core to the Main Ballroom where the reception had been set up. I was horrified to see all the Nobles gathered and applauding when Frank entered the room with me. Because I began screaming the word "traitors" over and over again, Frank had me brought up to my parents' room and locked me in while he stayed for the party.

I had been standing at the window for a while before realizing I was, yet again, living one of my visions. Thunder boomed and lightning struck a nearby tree as the tears freely flowed from my eyes. As the sky darkened to night, the rain fell harder, starting to flood the forest floor.

The longer I was alone, the more I dreaded the gradual silence overtaking the palace and streets of Petrichoria. When the door opened, I backed myself against the window. I was terrified, until I realized it was Phin. As soon as I realized who it was, I walked right up to him and slapped him across the face.

"You have some nerve coming here, Prince Phineas," I said coldly and turned to walk away.

"You look terrible, Rose," he said and grabbed my hand. Even though I hadn't seen a mirror, I knew I did. I was sure I had black lines dried onto my face from being streaked with tears and my hair no longer held the updo Adele had so lovingly put it into that morning. Frank tore the crown from my head in the hover when he tried to accost me and I had undone the braids subconsciously when I was sitting in the window.

"You may call me *Queen* Miriam," I said, snatching my hand back and spitting the title "Queen" out like a curse word. He had the gall to look hurt. "Do not look at me like that. You have no right."

"If you would let me explain," he said, grasping at me and catching my sleeve.

"Explain this: why bother having you win? Why didn't you just throw the test?"

"Two reasons. First, I was trying to convince Francis to let this go and let me have you. Second, if Francis *was* going to make me follow through, it was the only way to get my brother and his wife here so they could be assassinated."

"You make me sick. They were good people!"

"I have lived in my brother's shadow for so long. Francis offered to help Britainnia retake the east coast of this continent and it will be mine to rule."

Trying to pry his fingers from my sleeve, I said, "That is a terrible reason for your betrayal. What? Will you have your small nephew killed as well so you can take over Britainnia?" I finally got myself out of his grip and stumbled onto the floor from the force of the release. "You are a monster. Borderline worse than Frank."

"You have no idea what it has been like for me! I was never enough! Not for my parents. Not for George. Not for Britainnia. Then I come here and I'm not enough for you?! I couldn't take it anymore! It is *my* turn to be first!"

"You *lost*, Phin! What good is your gain of a kingdom if you are to rule it without love? I was to be your wife and you gave me away to a crazy man who was *happy* that I killed his father!"

"I feel *horrible* about all this, Rose!" He no longer shouted, but still spoke loudly and with fervency. "I didn't love you at first. I was toying with you, but – it changed. I tried to back out, but it was too late. I love you and my only comfort in all this is that you never loved me in return." By the end of his ridiculous monologue, his voice was soft.

"I *could* have loved you with time. Now, everyone in the world knows of your treachery and no woman would be stupid enough to trust you with her heart and no father or mother would dare give you their daughter!"

Phin looked stricken and taken aback at my outburst, but said nothing. Really, what could he say to that? It was all true – hurtful, but true. Looking at my hands holding me up on the floor, I said, "I think you had better go before *Francis* gets here. This will not be a pretty night for me." Returning my gaze to his, I said, "I will be sure to think of you as he rapes me tonight."

"I – I –" Phin could say nothing else and he left without another word, leaving me to await my wedding night of torture.

Chapter 35

When midnight rolled around, I began to think Frank wouldn't be coming. I knocked on the door from the inside and requested Adele's presence so I could go to sleep. The guard said nothing, but a little bit later, Adele was practically tossed into the room.

"Miriam!" Adele shouted and rushed me with a giant hug. "I saw the whole thing on your holocomm! I am so sorry about your parents and Peter and – I can't believe this is happening!"

I held onto her like she was my final lifeline. In fact, it really felt like she was. Yanking her by the hand, I pulled her into the bathroom and turned on the ventilation and faucets for the tub. "Tell me what's going on out there," I demanded as kindly as I could.

"There was rioting for a long time, but the streets are quiet. Rumor has it Frank tried to have the Delegates assassinated, but they were somehow warned about a possible coup and escaped."

"My parents must have warned the Delegates and Nobles about my vision. The Nobles are with Frank."

"I know. They're still at the reception in the Main Ballroom. I have to get you out of here."

"No. It's too dangerous. Find Earl and Louis. Find all the loyal Guards. Get somewhere safe."

"The loyal Guards are gone already – all but Louis. He refuses to leave. I will not abandon you, either, my Queen."

"You *must*. Find out where the Delegates and loyalists are hiding. Tell them I still fight. Tell them – tell them *they* must fight."

Adele nodded reluctantly. "As you command, Your Majesty." She turned to leave.

"Wait!"

Adele turned back. "What is it?"

"Get me out of this monstrosity!" We stared at each other for a moment, then burst out laughing. As she unbuttoned the dress and corset beneath, our laughing soon turned to crying again.

I stepped into the tub and Adele left before either of us could really say goodbye. As I settled into the tub and heard the door to the bedroom slide shut, it occurred to me that then I was absolutely, totally alone.

Though I really wanted to soak in the tub for the rest of the night, I loathed the idea of Frank finding me there, so I got out as soon as I was able to clean the death off my body and undo the rest of the braids in my hair so I could wash it, too.

Opening the door to the closet, I found all of Father and Mother's things gone. All of my things had been brought over and placed on one side of the closet and what I was assuming were Frank's things were where Father's had been before. I groaned in disgust, thinking that Frank's clothing had no place in the King and Queen's room.

I looked in my drawers, trying to find my long nightgowns, but found none. Naturally, Frank probably wanted me wearing one of the tiny nighties he put in there to make his job that evening easier. Smirking to myself, I nabbed a knit sweater and a pair of pull-on trousers and put them on. Father always said I was resourceful.

For the first time since being thrown into the room, I actually took a look around. Originally, I had just walked over and looked out the window. Then, I was only in the bathroom. Shaking my head, I wondered what happened to all of the beautiful furniture and blankets.

What Frank had put in the room wasn't *ugly*. It just wasn't what belonged in there. It infuriated me that he dared to have his own stuff brought to the palace and put in this room. That he had other people touch my things and move them. Of course, it *was* the same man who killed my parents, so nothing was probably off limits for him.

Pulling back the dark blue comforter, I climbed into the bed and shut off the lights. Rather than the normal comforting green light shining, the space needle let off a red glow. Knowing sleep would evade me when the beast arrived, I took advantage of the time I had by falling into a fitful sleep.

Standing at the entrance of the Main Ballroom, I watch the Nobles and Frank's followers dance and celebrate their takeover. It is not my normal premonition – it is a vision of what is going on right now.

Biting my thumbnail, I take in everyone present. Some people surprise me to see – like Robert Casey. I knew he was someone I could not trust. I wonder if Frank paid him to let him punch him or if he let him do it voluntarily.

Feeling a hand come up and remove my thumbnail from my mouth, I turn to my left and see David. He looks sad – as if he is feeling everything I feel. "Hello, David. I'm glad you're here."

Rather than release my hand, he entwines his fingers with mine and lowers our hands to our sides. "You need me," he says simply.

"I think Harrison must be awake. I am trying to bring him to me, but he doesn't show."

David simply nods in agreement.

Frank taps the side of a wine glass to signal he is beginning a speech. "Dukes and Duchesses of Arboria, welcome to this reception my lovely wife and her mother, God rest her soul, organized for the evening."

A few of the women titter at the joke at the expense of my dead mother. The wretches. I look at all the lovely flower arrangements and decorations. It feels like so long ago that Ella and I took the trip to the flower fields to decide on them – it was, actually. Ten years.

"Seriously though, I am sure Queen Miriam will come around eventually. I expect all of you to continue showing her the respect she deserves.

"The last of the original Noble families is finally dead. After much consideration, I have decided to appoint Robert Casey of Petrichoria as the new Duke of Maple."

Dumbfounded at the choice, I shake my head. Of all the men in the kingdom, he chose probably the worst of them. As Frank and Robert shake hands, I turn back to David. I didn't want to listen to Frank anymore.

I gesture towards Frank and say, "It was him all along."

"No. The Man of Night was his father first – before your freeze. He and Doctor Watson systematically had the Noble families killed and replaced with people loyal to their cause. That's why the Nobles

are all here celebrating. Frank only became in charge over the last few years."

"How do you know that?"

David frowns. "I don't know. Something tells me he didn't necessarily agree with all of Frank's methods, though. Probably why Frank was glad you killed him."

"None of this makes any sense. Why did they leave Peter and Ella alive ten years ago?"

"I have no idea, but I know Peter was meant to die with Ella and Tom in that hover explosion."

"You're probably right."

"You are afraid," David says. It is not a question. He knows. Of course, he does. He is me, after all.

"Frank is going to – do horrible things to me tonight."

"He has already done horrible things to you today. He had your parents killed and forced you to marry him."

I look back at him. "You know what I mean."

He looks back at me. "I do."

We both turn our attention back to the party-goers. "What is the point, David? Even with the warning, there was nothing I could do to save them."

"Your parents?"

"And George and Domoniue. And Peter. At least he's with Ella and Tom now. I feel terrible for thinking he could be a part of all this."

I think about his confession just before he died. There was no need to research it, I don't know how I accomplished the feat, but I really had spoken with Peter. He had been the one to open the chamber; probably the one who accidentally started my false life. More-than-likely, it was the reason David looked so much like him.

"You were probably responsible for saving the Delegates."

I shrug.

"There's nothing to be done about it now. Now, you move forward," David says.

"Where is Harrison tonight?"

David shrugs. "Probably losing his head going crazy trying to figure out a way to save you."

"You're probably right. He might be able to help, but I don't think he will be able to save me. Things are out of control in here in Arboria. And as its Queen, it is up to me to regain it."

Chapter 36

I woke to the feel of the blankets lifting behind me. My heart began racing and I began praying, silently, in earnest that Frank would not pursue anything. Pride and arrogance oozed from his pores and I could feel his ilk soak into my skin before he laid a hand on me.

Gently, he placed his fingertips on my shoulders and traced down my arms – to my hips – to my thighs – to my knees and calves. Frank chuckled at my makeshift pajamas. "Resourceful little minx. I know you're awake. Turn over."

Jerk. I am so *not his slave. I will* not *turn over voluntarily.*

Sighing, he said, "Rose, we can have an easy life or a hard life, which is it going to be?"

"Do you sincerely believe this is an easy life for me, *Francis*?" I asked, not turning over and making sure to emphasize his full name.

Resting his hand just above my elbow, he asked, "No more 'Frank?'"

"No," I choked on a sob and cleared my throat. "No. I think 'Frank' is dead. You are a monster, Francis."

"You're just upset, Rose. Turn over. Remember? You said when I became your betrothed, you would allow me to kiss you." He rubbed my arm in what was probably supposed to be a comforting way.

"That was long before you killed my parents."

"Come on, Rose. Turn over."

"I suppose it would be fruitless to tell you not to call me that."

"Yes. It would be. I will call you what I want now. Turn over."

"Did you and your fellow traitors enjoy the celebration of my parents' deaths?"

"We were not celebrating King Aaron and Queen Amoura's deaths. We were celebrating our marriage and ascension to the Crown. And we are not traitors. We are revolutionaries. Turn over."

I snorted sardonically. "Whatever you say, *Francis*."

Giving up on me turning over myself, he pulled my arm and repositioned me so I was facing him. Gaping, he said, "Roots. You look terrible."

"That's just what a girl wants to hear on her wedding night."

"You know what I mean."

I frowned and tried to push him away. "What did you expect, *Francis*? That you would kill my parents and I would be alright with it? There would be no tears shed? That I would throw myself into your arms and beg you to take me, *please*?"

He sighed exasperatingly. "Please call me 'Frank,' babe."

"Babe? That's a new one from you."

286

"Look, I knew you would be upset –"

" – try 'devastated' –"

" – and there would be tears –"

" – wracking sobs – "

Frank ran his fingers through my hair. " – but I expected you to have more strength –"

"*Francis*, how can I be strong when you have destroyed everything that gave me strength?"

"*I* did not kill your parents or anyone else you love."

"*You* ordered it. How is that not the same thing?"

We laid there looking into each other's eyes for a while. He was desperate for my love. I was angry with him and everything he had done.

Still rubbing my arm, he asked, "Aren't you warm in all those clothes?"

"Yes."

"Why don't you go change into actual night clothes, then?"

"Because nothing I would want to wear has been brought over. I don't feel comfortable wearing my dead mother's skimpy lingerie."

Frank rolled his eyes. "It is not your mother's lingerie. It's yours."

"It is precious – in a creepy way – that you think I am going to wear lingerie for you tonight."

"Is everything going to be a battle with you, Rose?"

"Yes."

"I am your King –"

"Technically, you haven't had your coronation yet."

"*Technically*, I did. Tonight. At the reception."

I shot myself out of the bed – too fast. Arms out to regain my balance, I intelligibly asked, "What? How? I wasn't present. The heir to the Crown has to be present in order for her spouse to be crowned King."

Frank casually got himself out of bed and I noticed he was only wearing boxer shorts. I closed my eyes and slammed my open palms over my eyes for good measure. He chuckled. Eyes on fire, I yelled, "Put some pants on, Frank!"

"Ah! You called me 'Frank!'"

"Whatever! Just do it!"

He didn't. Frank made his way over to me and grabbed at the hem of my sweater. Quickly, I ran to the other side of the room – straight into a corner, thanks to the fact my eyes were covered.

I threw my hands down. "Stupid corners," I muttered as Frank trapped me there.

"Hold on a moment," he said a couple feet away from me. Frank stood still with a frown on his face as the thought about something – really hard – it looked like it hurt. "How did you know about the coronation rules for the spouse of a reigning heir? How did you know *you* didn't personally need a coronation?"

Roots. I gave myself away.

"By all that is green and good. Rose, did you remember?" I stared at him blankly, hoping that the expression read "deer in hoverlights." "You did, didn't you? You got your memories back. Rose, that's great!" Frank took another step towards me and I pressed myself harder into my corner.

"But – that means you remember me, don't you?"

"We only met the one time, Frank – Francis."

"Frank. But you remember?"

"Yes."

Frank took another step, but I gave up on pressing any further into the wall. "Rose." He took another step and was only inches from me. Taking my hand gently in his, he breathed, "You remember me."

The way he was obsessing over it was weird. I had only met him the one time. He was a teenage boy and I was twenty. The way he was behaving, it was like we had an intimate relationship or something.

"Francis. We met once and you were significantly younger than me at the time. There were no romantic notions then."

"And now?" He wrapped his arm around my waist.

"Now, you are the man who killed my parents."

"Now, I am older than you and I am your King. As revolutionaries, we made an exception to the rule of you needing to be present for my crowning."

We were both breathing heavily – for different reasons. He was excited and I was scared. "Please, Frank. Don't do this."

"When you were my captive, you said you wouldn't sleep with me until we were married. We're married, Rose."

"I was saying and doing what I could to survive. I meant nothing I said."

"It doesn't change the fact that I want you. That I have wanted you for a very, *very* long time." With every word, his voice lowered and grew huskier.

At the risk of making things worse for myself, and hating how weak I felt, I lowered myself to my knees and gripped both of his hands in my quivering ones. With tears falling from my eyes, I tilted my head all the way back and drew his gaze to mine.

"I *beg* of you. Do not take my virginity from me this way. Please. Give me – time. Time to adjust to being Queen. Time to grieve the loss of my parents. Time to get used to the idea of being your wife. I will wear a nightgown. I will wear whatever you want. Just – don't *take* me. *Please*."

I felt low. I felt pathetic. I felt like anything but the Queen and woman I had been raised to be. There I was, begging a traitor not to rape me. I thought the first kiss interview was degrading, but in that moment, I felt destroyed.

Lowering my gaze to my knees, I waited for a response. For a moment, Frank just stood there, holding on to my trembling hands. Finally, he pulled me to standing and regarded me with regal eyes that I could no longer meet.

"How did that feel for you?" he asked.

"What?"

"Lowering yourself like that. How do you feel?"

"Horrible," I muttered. "Like nothing."

"You feel that desperately about this?" Frank tilted my chin so I had no choice but to look at his eyes.

Blinking furiously, I swallowed before answering his question. "Yes."

Nodding once, he stepped away and walked out of the room. After the door shut behind him, I stared at the empty space that he had previously occupied. Slowly, I made my way back over to the giant bed.

What just happened? Is he coming back?

I sat on the edge of the bed and stared at the door for several minutes. Something told me he *would* be coming back.

When he returned a bit later, his arms were full of my night clothes. As if presenting an offering, he laid the pile before me. "Here are all your nightgowns, Rose."

I looked at him with wide eyes. "Thank you?"

"Wear anything you like."

Hesitantly, I bent over and selected my favorite long satin nightgown and lifted it from the stack. "Go on," Frank said, gesturing toward the bathroom.

"I can change into this? Without you watching?"

"Yes."

"What's the catch?"

"Don't wear day clothes to bed. Especially clothes like this. It's – weird."

"What?"

"Go change, Rose. I will not force myself on you tonight."

"Tonight?"

Frank chuckled. "I would rather not force myself on you *any* night, but I am only so patient. I will give you until Christmas night to get yourself situated and figured out."

"You want to ruin Christmas for me?"

Frank sighed and looked at the ceiling. "Would you rather just get it over with tonight? Because I *really* want it tonight. I have been waiting a long time for this. Literally *sleeping* with my wife is not how I imagined my wedding night."

I stared at him. "This isn't exactly how I imagined my wedding night either," I said quietly.

Continuing to stare at him, I considered his offer. Until he had my parents killed, I had never doubted that Frank was in love with me. Perhaps my begging demonstrated I was willing to part with a portion of my pride for certain – things. Perhaps that meant something to him.

"You *are* a virgin, then?" he asked. Frank had asked me that before, in a teasing way, when I was his prisoner. I didn't know then. At that moment, with the two of us alone in the room, I did.

"Yes."

Frank looked at the pile of nightgowns. "I'm not." He didn't sound proud about it. In fact, he sounded ashamed. Breathing out slowly, he said, "Rose, Christmas is two weeks away. If it wasn't me, it was going to be Phineas, who you are not in love with either, right?"

I nodded slowly.

Scratching his eyebrow, he looked to me again. "I can pretty much guarantee you that he would not have given you *any* time to adjust."

"Having seen his selfish side today, I don't think you are wrong."

Will it be long enough for someone to rescue me or for me to escape? I don't have a choice, really. I have to take what I can get.

"Alright, Frank. Christmas." He smiled widely at me. "But don't expect anything magical. After today, I don't know that there is *any* chance I will *ever* fall in love with you."

Lie. Indeed, I do know that I will never fall in love with you, you monster.

"I won't." Frank stood and offered me his hand. "You *will* share a bed with me, though." I nodded submissively and allowed him to help me stand.

The more submissively I behave, the easier it will be to escape.

"Alright. While you change, I will put these in your drawer with the lingerie," Frank said. Hearing him say the word "lingerie" made me feel like I just took a dip in a giant mud puddle. Again, I nodded submissively and went to the bathroom to change.

Closing the door behind me, I looked in the mirror. My eyes were red and puffy from crying – alright – and begging. I took the hot sweater and trousers off and slid the nightgown over my head. After running the brush through my hair again, I walked out of the bathroom into the red light of the bedroom.

The stack of nightgowns was no longer in the middle of the room. Because I couldn't see Frank, I assumed he was in the closet putting the clothes away like he said he would.

When he padded out of the closet, still only in his boxers, he stalled upon seeing me in my nightgown. I was under no illusion that he was sane or someone who kept his word at all, so I paused when he did.

With a smirk, Frank strolled over to my side of the bed and pulled the blankets back for me. Cautiously, I walked over and sat down on the sheet. Rolling his eyes, he lowered himself to his knees again, lifted my legs and tucked them into the blankets.

He moved to get in on his side and I pulled the blankets up to my chin. After he was in, he didn't ask me to turn over, he just scooted over so his chest was to my back and wrapped an arm around me.

Quietly, I asked, "Why are you being so agreeable with me?"

Stroking my hair with his free hand, he said, "Because I love you, Rose."

We lay there in silence for a while before I broke it. "Just so you know, I am not giving up on Arboria."

Frank stopped stroking my hair and hovered so his lips were over my ear. "Just so you know, neither am I."

Acknowledgements

First, and foremost, I would like to thank God for everything He has done for me. Most specifically, I thank Him for His inspiration and gift of writing.

I would not have been able to write this first novel, or the rest of the Rose of Petrichoria series, without the support of my family at The Barn. Thank you for all your encouragement and love! My husband, Nick, was gracious enough to let me use his idea of the Daze for the pandemic in this series. Be looking forward to a couple prequels where it plays a more prominent role.

Several people read through and critiqued Remembered and I am appreciative for all of you, too: Julie Hauenstein, Lynnette Bonner, Becky Luna, Sheri Mast, Deborah Wyatt, and Cara Koch.

Note From The Author

Forgetting your life, or knowing someone who has, is a horrible experience. In 2007, my mother suffered strokes while recovering from quadruple bypass heart surgery. One of the debilitating consequences was a loss of short-term memory. Over time, her vascular dementia has progressed to the point that she most often doesn't remember most long-term memories either.

If you have a loved one who is living with dementia, it is understandable that it would be difficult to see them go through it, or even to experience the heartbreak when they don't recognize you. People with dementia don't have the luxury of remembering your last visit. They live in the here and now. While it may be hard for you to see them, give them the love and respect they continue to deserve because they are still human beings with human feelings.

They have forgotten, do not forget them.

About The Author

Katie Hauenstein was educated at Northwest University in Kirkland, Washington, where she met and married her husband, Nick Hauenstein. After graduating with her Bachelor's Degree in Communication, she had her daughter, Mary, and began writing her stories. Forgotten, the first book in the Rose of Petrichoria series, is her first published novel.

In her spare time, you can find Katie binge watching superhero/sci-fi/fantasy shows on Netflix, fangirling about Doctor Who, attending a variety of movies at the local theater, or with her nose in a book. She also enjoys cake decorating, online shopping, and other introverted activities.